RHINE JOURNEY

HOLT, RINEHART AN

ANN SCHLEE

Rhine Journey

A NOVEL

WINSTON · NEW YORK

First published in January 1981 by Holt, Rinehart and Winston,
383 Madison Avenue, New York, New York 10017.

Library of Congress Cataloging in Publication Data
Schlee, Ann.
Rhine journey.
I. Title.
PZ4.S339Rh 1980   [PR6069.C514]   823'.914   80-12265
ISBN: 0-03-056894-3

Designer: Amy Hill
First Edition
Printed in the United States of America
1 3 5 7 9 10 8 6 4 2

*To my companions on the Rhine
in the summer of 1977*

RHINE JOURNEY

HISTORICAL NOTE

Visitors to Rhenish Prussia, in the summer of 1851, found much to charm them. They also found much to condemn. The British particularly, always so mindful of their own national liberties, railed against the power of the Prussian police, the censorship of the press, the restrictions placed on the Lutheran Church.

Many citizens of the Rhineland would have agreed with them and felt bitterly that the aftermath of the 1848 revolutions had seen the curtailment of those freedoms they had hoped to extend. Some of the more outspoken critics of Frederick Wilhelm IV's regime found themselves under threat of arrest.

Karl Marx had fled from Cologne in 1848 and settled in London the following year. When a fellow member of the Communist League escaped from prison in 1850, Frederick Wilhelm urged his Prime Minister to intensify the government's attack on the workers' movement. Rumours were spread of an international revolutionary plot centred on the Great Exhibition. Ports and railway stations were carefully watched for subversive workers seeking to escape to England. By June the majority of the League was under arrest and was brought to trial in Cologne in October of 1852.

It is unlikely that the Morrison family was concerned or even aware of these events. They had come for Marion's sake, to take the waters at Baden Baden and to experience on their return a romantic Rhine composed mostly of the fruits of judicious reading and the play of their own imaginations. But it is against the background of these events that their summer excursion is set.

The Landing Stage
at Coblenz

'The luggage has simply been left on the deck,' said the Reverend Charles Morrison. 'I had thought, Charlotte, that you were with it.'

Charlotte, his sister for whose summer excursion (the fact suffused her at this moment) he had generously paid, said, 'Surely you didn't ask me.'

'Was it necessary to ask? I assumed that when you went off by yourself on to the deck it was to check on the luggage, knowing as you did that I was otherwise occupied.'

For he had been distributing tracts for the edification of their fellow passengers. She could not restrain a glance at the black velvet bag slung across his shoulder, nor repress her sensation of relief that it was empty. She said of the luggage, 'I'm sure it is quite safe.'

'On the contrary, you have no occasion to be sure of any such thing. We have been warned often enough of thieving on the Rhine and have observed the extreme negligence of the shipowners. I have impressed upon you before, Charlotte, the possibility that the captain may actually be in league with the thieves. It is our duty to be vigilant at all times over the property of others as well as our own.'

She loved him, had always loved him, but knew him to be habitually thus, like a lantern swung deliberately on a pole, searching in this part, then in that, going over the matter a second time. Had it not been the luggage it would have been something else. Soon he would mention the Almighty. She looked swiftly away from his face to the approaching town of Coblenz. Thick yellow walls glowing in the late sun seemed to skim towards them propped precariously on their unsteady yellow reflections. But she dared not look away long.

'The Almighty after all asks us to help ourselves in the first instance. Then when we have measured our ineptitude to the hilt, He intervenes with His grace.'

'But what,' she asked carefully, 'would you like me to do about the luggage now?'

Nothing could quicken the pace of Mr Morrison's arguments. The deck listed with the weight of passengers straining against the shoreward rail. Some of them, she noticed, waved towards the approaching shore with their tracts. Others used them as fans, for the evening was sultry. Though many, she told herself, would have been carefully folded and placed in reticule or coattail pocket for later earnest perusal. Devoutly she hoped that he had not seen the one or two that had fluttered past them on the deck. But he had not.

He stood alone with his back to the town. Strands of grey hair blew from under the brim of his hat. His strong plain face was as deeply weathered as any of the farm labourers' to whom he ministered. His blue eyes were set fixedly on some place where no one, to Charlotte's knowledge, was ever permitted to land. He continued to expound the grace of God until it occurred to her that he was frightened at the thought of yet another new place and needed consolation.

She laid her hand on his arm and said, 'I shall go and check that it is safe, if you will find Marion and Ellie and say that we have arrived.'

Confronted with a duty, immediately he went and she was left on a deck too congested with the wide dark skirts of the lady passengers for her to press on to the pile of luggage forward of the mast. But, optimistic by nature, trained in the belief that people left in charge of things were infallible, she had no fears at all that the strong young men surrounding the luggage with ropes would fail to lower it over the side, where subsequently they would find it.

A space occurred near her at the rail. She fitted herself into it, placed her gloved hands side by side on the polished wood of the rail, and stared down at the scene below.

It was at that moment – when the throb and vibration of the engine ceased, the brass bell jangled their arrival, and the steamer made its shuddering contact with the land – that Charlotte felt a sudden intense pain in what she had been taught to believe was her heart.

The crowd on the shore stared upwards at the passengers. At one moment their faces were no more than pale shapes among the white scarves of the peasant women and a cluster of spiked brass helmets flashing in the last of that day's sun; at the next, eyes, mouths became distinct, upturned, searching. Then pain brought tears to the eyes so that the whole scene wavered and started on a course of disintegration, as if invisible fumes off some rising conflagration had drifted between herself and the shore. All this because near the space cleared for the gangplank, she had seen, for the first time in twenty years, the face of a man called Desmond Fermer.

She gripped the rail in an astonishment of pain. In recent years, reaching in moments of self-pity for her broken heart, she had felt little or no sensation, and now without warning the long bandaging years were cruelly stripped away at the sight of a black coat, a tall hat, a heavy handsome face staring up, it appeared, at her.

Of course it was not he. She had known this at once. This man was her own age, forty-five at the most. Desmond Fermer would be by now sixty, aging, stout, grey, perhaps dead after all. Knowing that it was not he, she knew that he was not looking at her. That now, raising his hat, smiling, shouting sounds which were lost among the shouts of the men securing the gangplank, with his eyes fixed seemingly onto hers, that it could not be she that he saw.

Instantly by her shoulder, a woman's voice called in English, 'Here, Edward, here,' and turning she saw a stout, comely lady backed by two tall sons waving in reply. Her husband. Other people. No matter.

Legs moved on command. They remembered the raised sill into the cabin; 'I do beg your pardon,' to the Frenchwoman she brushed against. In the crowded cabin a row of ladies leant towards the long pier glass that encircled the wall. Their skirts tilted up behind them and although they talked to one another their faces were intent. Their reflected hands moved briskly about imperceptible adjustments. Charlotte moved in among them and there appeared in front of her what she had learned to accept was

6

her face. She stared at it dispassionately, wondering if it yet showed any sign of the disintegration she had felt inside herself. Apparently not. Apparently she flashed the same signal to the world as she had on all previous days—dark eyes, smooth hair, straight nose, neat bonnet, saying in effect, 'Respect me, but let me pass.'

When suddenly her sister-in-law's face appeared beside hers in the glass it seemed more familiar than her own, more closely watched over the years.

'There you are,' said Marion's voice and Charlotte, alive at once to its minutest emphasis, said without turning, 'Yes, I was watching us land.'

She watched Marion stare at herself, open-eyed, her chin folded softly in, as she performed those automatic pointless actions (they were being repeated all around the cabin) with which one prepares to meet new places; a tug at each side of the collar, the hair smoothed out under the bonnet's brim, the rapid pulling of each glove finger's end, and all the time her little mouth worked in her soft round face.

The hotel frontage looked quite respectable. But might it not be noisy by the river? Still, if it were clean on the outside might it not be clean on the inside? So long as there was no repetition of Heidelberg. She did not think, tucking in the folded chin, turning the head, pursing the lips, that Charles's nerves would stand another such ordeal. Charlotte felt strengthened by these certainties. She thought, I have been absurd, and said softly, 'And you, dear, how are you feeling? I have found no chance to ask you today.'

'Tired, of course,' said Marion with her sweet resignation. The reflected eyes fastened onto Charlotte's and the little mouth gave a tight quick smile. 'But then there are so many things of more moment than how I feel.'

To this of course, there is no answer, only the need to

make a move. Everything when one is travelling must be gone over bead by bead. Gloves, shawl, reticule, Marion's checked travelling rug, her red guidebook to be collected off the red plush seat. She followed Marion across the cabin. 'Remember the sill,' she said, reaching out to touch her lightly on the shoulder.

Already the passengers were making their slow way down the gangplank. Luggage swung on ropes. It is impossible not to hope at the prospect of such newness, not to crane to see the hotel with its bold lettering between the rows of windows, not to look down again at the crowd on the quay, shifted now like the pattern in a kaleidoscope, and freed of ghosts.

Ahead of her Marion raised herself on tiptoe to look first over one shoulder of the gentleman in front of her, then over the other. Her gloved hand darted over her head.

'Have you seen them?'

'I thought I had. Yes, there they are.' She called out to her husband and daughter, in a little voice they could not hear, 'Charles, Ellie.' But they were caught in different streams slowly converging on the top of the gangplank. 'What the hurry is,' said Marion, 'I shall never know,' but she stood on tiptoe again and darted up her hand as if she might force her way past the solid black back that blocked her.

Now Charlotte could see them too; her brother with his hair blowing in the wind and his mouth clamped shut on inconceivable thoughts, and straining from his side Ellie, her niece—but in her heart her child—with her bright hair escaping from under the edge of her bonnet, alive, alight, sucking in life from everyone around her, crying out as they were borne slowly towards one another, 'Oh, Charlotte, look at the bridge.' So that when they met at the head of the gangplank Charlotte found herself being

drawn back by Ellie's strong warm hand to the bows of the
steamer.

'Charlotte,' she said warmly in her aunt's ear, 'I feel so
strange.'

'Why is that?'

'It's this place.'

'But we have only just arrived.'

'I know. Don't you feel it?'

'No,' said Charlotte. 'Places begin to seem alike.'

'Aren't you happy? Aren't you enjoying it?' She was
stricken.

'Yes. Of course.'

'Well then, can't you feel something?'

'Only that this is a new place.'

'I have the strangest feeling that something will happen
to me here. I shouldn't say so even to you, because nothing
ever really happens and you will be sure to laugh at me
when we go away again, but it came to me all of a sudden
when the boat came into the side and everyone was looking up at us, that they'd come especially to meet me and
that I was looking for a face that would make sense of it.'
At that she was overcome with her own foolishness and
hid her face between her aunt's neck and shoulder.

But Charlotte was disposed to be serious. 'Did you see
such a face?'

'No, of course not.' But then she insisted, 'Tell me, do
you ever think of this one moment? Now. This is me now.
This is happening to me.'

'Not any more.'

'Oh, you make yourself out so old.'

But Charlotte could remember just that, standing at the
centre of the universe on the very apex of time. Now it
seemed that she stood a little to the side of centre and that
her awareness was not confined to any particular moment.

.

9

.

Lights were going on in the town, giving it depth, a suggestion of back streets and lives suddenly illuminated in the moment before the curtains are drawn. Once tiny filaments would have connected her to all those windows, to all those lives. But now she knew those streets to be composed of a dense element, nonconductive of spirit, which she would penetrate and emerge from gratefully without influencing or being influenced. But Ellie must still believe that the town reacted and attracted, wanted to take from her and to give.

They were standing now in the very bows of the steamer. A cold, wild river smell surrounded them. To the left lay a cluster of small boats, by the landing stage. Behind them the bland white façades of the hotels rose above the yellow city walls. Directly ahead was what Ellie had brought her to see. A line of flat barges with the roadway laid over it, crowded at this evening hour with peasants returning from market. They could see the white scarves of the women, the empty knapsacks sagging on the backs of the men as they moved towards the farther shore, whilst working its way against them was an eddy of blue uniforms, the bright helmets of the officers and men coming down from the fortress of Ehrenbreitstein to pass the evening in the town.

'Oh, I wish we had been going the other way,' said Ellie. 'Then they would have had to open for us.' And because the world that summer seemed to conspire to give her exactly what she wanted, a gun sounded from the bank, causing them both to start and clasp their hands more closely together.

'Oh, look, look,' cried Ellie, for the barriers were down and the stream of people halted congested behind them. The central boats separated. The strong brown river was triumphant between them, and working up against the current they saw a little steamer like their own, coming perhaps from Cologne, where a week from now they would reach the climax of their tour.

They stood watching until the steamer passed and the bridge closed. Then, still hand in hand, they retraced their steps and walked down the gangplank into the waiting town.

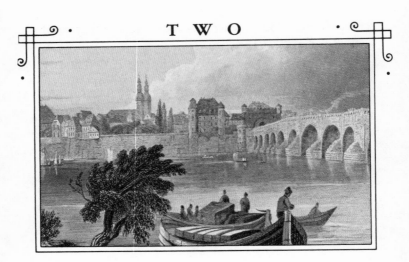

The Table d'Hôte

No need to ask my name. No need to make discreet enquiries after my circumstances; to wonder where I live, what class of company I keep, or all those essentials that the world must know before it can make up its mind to like or dislike. No, I am simply the woman opposite to you in the diligence to Basle; three places away at the table d'hôte at Heidelberg. You must like or dislike on impulse for tomorrow I am gone. So quickly enjoy my fine grey eyes which people still admire; my quiet self-effacing nature which will not permit me to raise my voice, nor demand the window be opened, nor press upon you my opinion of the view.

In return I would ask you not to speculate on whether my handsome brown silk were a gift from my sister-in-law, cut down *in haste to fit my less ample form, nor if the hand in my neat glove be ringed or unringed. Believe me if you will a comfortable widow, and the bright face at my side—which does, they say, a little resemble mine—my daughter perhaps. Do not question and let me pass.*

So Charlotte Morrison: to her journal at an early halt in their tour, when all the freshness of the journey was still upon her and the cares and duties of her former life still sufficiently real in memory for her to be delightfully aware of their absence. She woke each morning with a sense of their weight which had settled again perhaps in dreams, only to feel it lift and vanish so that she lay afloat with very lightness above the surface of the bed, her mind unable to imagine the sights they would visit during that day.

Only on that first night in Coblenz, seeing herself haunt the corner of a glass given over to charms of Ellie's brushing out her hair, did she suddenly long for the safe confines of home, the hard edges of her old identity.

She sat a little behind the dressing table, by an open window, stitching a cloth button to the waistband of Ellie's petticoat. Within the hour a bell would ring and they must face the descent to the table d'hôte. Faces would raise indifferently and, not recognising, turn away. On that evening for the first time she wished that they might know her at once for Miss Morrison.

Miss Morrison whose brother held the living at Melbury, who had acted for twenty years as housekeeper to the Reverend and very elderly Mr Ransome at Ditchbourne and nursed him before his death; frail, dying old man who had locked his bone fingers about hers and asked her if she loved him. 'Yes,' said Miss Morrison. 'I love you.' In the circumstances it had been true enough to say.

Miss Morrison who walked about the village with a

·

13

·

round willow basket on her arm, who taught in the school, who was tolerated by the poor for some quality of poverty they sensed in her, who sometimes so forgot herself as to laugh aloud when she had occasion to chase the hens in from the lane.

This person Charlotte knew to be not entirely herself, but had been agreed upon by persons whose pressures she missed. For it seemed in a sudden morbid fancy that it was only along the line where she felt those particular pressures that she knew herself to begin. So she stitched her button. In less than two weeks they would be home, but even that word must be thought with caution. Old Mr Ransome had, it was found, left her an independence, but he had taken with him her abode and her occupation. She wound the cotton around and around the shank. Who she was to be and where she was to live had somehow to be agreed upon.

She was not herself. The sight of that face on the quay had jarred her deeply, for what was she to him or he, a total stranger, to her? Nor were those sensations of pain caused by the memory of physical violence done twenty years ago to something virginal and unresolved: the parting in the parlour at the mill; the sound of the water, nothing said, nothing admitted. Rather they seemed an acknowledgement now that it had been as she had felt it to be. Not as others had told her it was. So that there was a danger of her thinking, if that were real then so might . . . She bent her head and bit the thread.

It is one of the chief consolations of family life that such thoughts never penetrate to their conclusions. Always there is an interruption, or how quickly the whole structure of things would be undermined. It was necessary to eat again, to prepare for their appearance at the table d'hôte.

·

·

Now Ellie from the dressing table said suddenly, 'I am tired. I don't want to go down.' So she too feared the descent of the stairs, the upturned faces, the unknown words. All the more reason to lean forward on the little gilt chair and say pleasantly, 'But this was to be such a special place for you.'

'I knew you would laugh at me if I said that. It was just foolishness. Nothing ever happens.'

'Do you feel unwell?' For she did look a little pale.

'Only Mama is allowed to feel unwell.'

'Oh, Ellie! How can you!' Now she was simply tiresome.

'You don't mind her. You put up with anything. I suppose you have to.'

She let that pass. She did not speak at all, but came and stood behind her niece, resting her hands on the back of her chair and watching. Ellie slid her two hands up her face and clutched back the ravel wool hair that spread thickly on her shoulders. 'I'll go down if I may wear my hair up. Well?' she said, turning defiantly to Charlotte, who had not answered.

'You must ask your mama.'

'I am asking you. I am asking what you say. Don't you think it looks very much nicer up?' And she turned back, pouting approval at her reflection.

'No. I like you as you are.'

Her look of scorn glanced off the mirror.

'Well, ask your mother then.'

'Oh, why?'

'You only don't because you know she will say no.'

'You could take my side.'

'Oh, Ellie, don't upset her. Don't spoil things for her.'

'Why should it spoil things for her to make me happy?' But her voice, begun almost in a passion, died away. They both had heard the door of the outer salon open. A mo-

.

15

.

ment later they watched the brass door handle of their bedroom turn. Ellie's mother entered the room.

She was dressed for dinner in a dark silk gown; a woman Charlotte knew to be in her fifties; but who, not knowing, would suspect that? Her beautiful hair was scarcely faded from the deep coppery colour she had bequeathed to her daughter. Plumpness which in her youth had made her appear older than her years now made her seem younger. The full round cheeks and chin showed little trace of sagging or wrinkling, only under her eyes fine clear skin gathered like a tiny swag of muslin, giving a surprised, slightly comic look, quite at odds with the set of her determined little mouth.

'Are you both ready?'

Her very presence in the room effected a safe return to the rightful balance of power. Charlotte withdrew, as she spoke, to her seat by the window and lifted automatically the petticoat although her task upon it was done. She said, 'Ellie has been asking if she may wear her hair high.'

'Why especially tonight?' Marion Morrison leant past her daughter to straighten the accoutrements of the dressing table, and seeing her sister-in-law in the mirror said, 'You are not, I hope, doing her mending for her. She is well able to do it herself. You are not to act the poor relative among us, Charlotte dear, especially as you no longer are.'

'I'd like it for a change,' said Ellie.

'Doesn't being in a new place every day satisfy you? It is quite enough for me.'

'But your hair is up.'

'Well, I can hardly let it down at my age.' Her laugh was light and charming. It included Charlotte in a conspiracy of wisdom. She was a woman that other women liked. Charlotte had often noticed.

Actual tears had risen in Ellie's eyes. 'I am seventeen.'

'I was aware,' said her mother.

'Sarah Wentworth wore her hair up at seventeen. Everybody does.'

'Everybody is not my daughter.'

'Oh, never mind,' cried Ellie and sweeping angrily the litter of pins and combs on the table before her, she sank her head abruptly onto her arms.

'How long has she been like this?' said Marion coldly.

Charlotte from her corner said, 'She's tired.'

'I'm not tired.'

'Perhaps it would be better if she did not come down tonight,' pleaded Charlotte. 'I could stay with her.'

But that was not what Ellie wanted either. She turned her head sideways on her arm and looked cautiously out at her mother.

'Of course she will accompany us. She says she is not tired but even if she were, all women must learn to hide their little fatigues and vexations' – and here she slid the very tips of her fingers across her brow as if in an unconscious indication of just such a hiding place.

'Perhaps I shall permit you to wear your hair high for tonight if only to remind you that you cannot still hope to act the child to win sympathy. I shall dress it and I shall hope to see you bear yourself in such a way so as not to seem a little girl dressed up.'

She set about her task with lips pursed and soft chin drawn in. They all watched gravely as the rite was performed; the hair coiled and pinned. They saw the little mirrored face drawn out from its bright protective thicket. They watched it shed its residue of childhood, grow pointed, and take on a contained and waiting look.

It seemed to Charlotte to be a cruel error; a transformation of whatever was exceptional in Ellie into something without mystery that everyone might interpret at a glance.

·

·

At any moment Marion would surely put a stop to it, but glancing at her sister-in-law she saw instead of disapproval a rapt and satisfied look. When all was done she smiled and clapped her hands softly together. 'Turn around,' she cried gaily and then, though she did not consult Charlotte by so much as a glance, it must be to her that she added in an indulgent tone, 'It can do no harm. It is not as if we were known here. Come turn around and let us admire you.'

Ellie, awed out of ill temper, turned shyly to face them.

'Ah,' said her mother, turning to one side with a rapid calculating look. 'Ah.' For some reason she was immensely pleased. She reached out a hand and curved it against Ellie's cheek. The gesture was unlike a touch applied to a person, but rather to some artifact that had turned out well, and so too the look of satisfaction. So that Ellie blushed and lowered her eyes.

'Well, Charlotte?'

'I liked her as she was before.'

'Oh, Charlotte, how cross you are,' cried Ellie and, perhaps to break away from something in her mother's face, she stood up, and running to Charlotte threw her arms impulsively around her neck.

Marion cried out, 'Oh, you will spoil it!'

But Charlotte softened, forgave. It was only for tonight.

'What will Papa say?'

'I shall tell him,' said Marion collectedly. 'I shall let him take me down first. Then he will have to contain himself during the meal by which time he will probably have become accustomed to the idea. Light the lamp,' she said to Charlotte as she left. 'It is growing dark in here.'

But as if by silent agreement they did not. The room fell quiet after her departure. It was pleasant to watch the clear summer light enter the room and move like an intruder along the walls and into the corners before it ventured into the centre of the room. The mirror was too shadowy to confront them. They sat side by side, Charlotte on her chair, Ellie on the floor beside her with her white skirt spread carefully out, staring at the high shuttered façade of the house opposite, and felt disposed by feelings of newness and strangeness, to talk to one another.

'I'm sure Mama let you wear your hair high when you were seventeen.'

'I was not her child. She was less protective of me.' Then hearing herself, she quickly added, 'We were more like sisters.'

'But how old were you?' For that was what mattered.

'Fifteen.' Her smile, sad and amused at the memory of herself, was drawn out into the dark where it was intended.

'Fifteen!'

'Ah, but Ellie. It was all so different. Besides, it was nothing to do with your mama. We had not met her then, although we were to that night. It was at that dance at Melbury where your mama and papa met one another.'

'Tell me,' said Ellie, and reaching into Charlotte's lap she took tight hold of her hands.

'But you know it already. You must.'

'Tell me,' she demanded, for tonight she was a new person and must learn it afresh.

Charlotte, after keeping silent for a moment, was glad enough to comply, for these are the seminal tales that must be told again and again. Each time they lose a little of their potency. They become mere fictions. They are pushed away. One does not tell them as one speaks, but as if they were read from a book. One thinks, I have triumphed now. That couldn't hurt me now, and indeed the ghost of Desmond Fermer staring up at her from the quay had only the power to hurt for minutes, and that was because of the unexpectedness of the sight. So she began:

.

19

.

'Your father held the curacy then under Mr Walker, but we lived at Peaslake and I kept house for him on sixty pounds a year. I laugh now to think of our economies but then it was earnest enough. There was to be a dance at Melbury House. Your Aunt Mary had become engaged and for the first time your father and I were invited, I suppose at Mr Walker's behest for he was growing old and wanted your father to follow him and thought, I suppose, that we should be brought out more into the local society. At any event the invitation was sent. At first your papa said we should not go because you know he has always thought it very wrong for gentlemen and ladies to dance with one another. I thought I was sorry not to go and to miss all the fine people, but then the Rector prevailed upon him and promised that he would not be called upon to dance, only to be present, and he agreed. Of course I must do as I pleased. Strangely, once it was real, I was very afraid.'

'Why?' said Ellie, as if she encouraged that younger girl. 'You said you wanted to go.'

Charlotte did not so much reply as steadily resume her narrative.

'I had never been in company of any account and had little idea how to conduct myself, for you see when I accompanied him in the parishes, as I always did, I was his sister and the love which people felt for him even as a young man was extended to me. I never had to win it for myself or to appear on my own.'

'And the dress?' For there was a danger that her aunt might run on to unessentials.

'I had no dress remotely suitable. In the end Mrs Walker said that she could provide an old one of her daughter's. Whether it would fit me or in any way become me there was no means of telling, but I was satisfied enough that she called it an evening dress. I found our father's old evening coat and sponged it and pressed it for your papa and on the

Friday we wrapped it in paper and set out to walk the five miles to Melbury.

'Mrs Walker provided us with rooms at the Rectory and brushed and pinned me into some semblance of order. First she pinned my hair up, but I was unlike you, Ellie. I hated to feel so strange when everything about me was strange. I begged her to let it down again. She brushed it out and sighed and said no, she thought it had looked better up. I was too in awe of her to protest more. When all was done, she sighed again and said, yes, she thought that was better, but I sensed that she was displeased with me, and felt more wretched than ever. At the last she cried out, "But your shoes. You have forgotten to change your shoes."

'I said, "I have no others," for under the borrowed dress I still wore the stout shoes in which I had walked over the hills from Peaslake.'

'What did she do? Did she lend you dancing shoes?'

'No. I think at that point she despaired of me. She merely looked vexed and said that as she was sure my brother would not permit me to dance it scarcely mattered, only she begged me to take very little steps so that no one would see, and made me take a turn about the room for practice. Really I suppose it was very good of her to take such trouble over me when no doubt she had troubles of her own with Mr Walker failing and three daughters of marriageable age. The party must have been a great event in their lives. But at the time I felt she tormented me. I wanted to run away. As she went downstairs she turned to me and said in a cross whisper, "Try at least to look less miserable." And that of course made my misery complete.'

'I'm sure you looked pretty really,' said Ellie anxiously; she turned back to the darkened glass as if she would have run to it for her own reassurance.

There was a light tapping on the outer door. In a minute or two they must follow. Charlotte laughed and said,

'How little it seems to matter now,' but she remembered that it had mattered then or had seemed to.

Ellie was already on her feet, smoothing out her skirt with a little frown of concentration. In the long hotel corridor she clung to Charlotte's arm. In a sudden passion of anxiety, she whispered, 'Does it look all right? Is it really all right?'

'Yes. Yes,' said Charlotte, patting her hand. 'I like it really.'

As they came out on the landing, she felt Ellie stiffen and detach herself from all but the lightest pressure on her arm. They were visible now from the room below. The diners looked up, saw that glowing face set against the aunt's dark shoulder, caught the resemblance, and would have thought them mother and daughter or even sisters, for Charlotte moved with an impatience and paused with an uncertainty that made people suppose her younger than she was. Only the lack of restraint between them as they descended the stairs suggested a more distant relationship.

This was the largest hotel in which they had yet stayed. They planned to spend three or four more days here for the expeditions. 'Oh, it is the grandest yet, grander even than Baden Baden,' whispered Ellie, staring straight ahead of her.

Music pumped cheerfully from a little orchestra in a musicians' gallery. A fountain in a niche sparkled amid a small jungle of plants and no less than three tables ran the length of the room. Already they were nearly filled with diners whose babel of voices fought with the music.

Charlotte could make out the merry party of French people who had trailed them from Basle. German families from the town squeezed in with no apparent resentment beside their former conquerors, though a few must remember Napoleon's soldiers in the streets of their childhood, an elder brother, perhaps, conscripted for the Eastern campaign. And there in a solid block of blue, their successors at the fort of Ehrenbreitstein, the handsome young Prussian officers, puffing vilely on cigars as they ate; their swords and helmets arming an entire hat stand at the foot of the stairs.

On which aunt and niece now paused; the aunt to peer around for Ellie's parents; the niece holding her rapt, waiting face a little to the light, feeling the eyes and unknown words beat softly upon her like rain, focusing on nothing and no one.

'Why, there they are,' cried Charlotte.

As soon as they saw Mr Morrison they were very aware of his eye upon them. He sat upright at the long crowded table. His grey hair fell straight to his collar. His face was creased with an austere concern. Two vacant seats opposite were turned with their backs to the table. Not until they were seated could he speak without raising his voice.

'You look very fine, my dear.'

The words were not entirely without censure, but his tone was almost kind. Ellie blushed painfully, lowered her eyes, then raised them above her father's head as if she had not been addressed. But there was no need for conversation. The business of eating pressed in on them. They worked in silence at their unsympathetic beef, which held, Mr Morrison presently remarked, no resemblance to English beef; though all beasts came from the same stock after the Inundation.

All around them was the sound of human gaiety and they were surely a part of it. His statement had been intended as final, but Charlotte was moved to take him up on it. 'But not all nations,' she said, pitching her voice to the sounds around her. 'You are tasting the vast superiority of English cooks.'

Her brother made no response and she felt at once that she had spoken excessively. But why should she not speak?

Recklessly she turned to the Frenchwoman next to her, knowing that her brother at least had not forgiven the French. His disapproval rather than her neighbour's delightful smile and bow of response provoked her into bad French. Were they staying long at Coblenz? Had they enjoyed themselves today?

But yes. They had enjoyed themselves immensely. They had taken a carriage to Stolzenfels and ridden up to see the castle. On donkeys, Madame, such delicious little donkeys and the view was *ravissante*. Her eyebrows rose to uncanny heights at the memory.

'Donkeys, Ellie! Do you hear? Shall we go?'

'Le place pour s'enivrer des charmes du Rhin,' declared the little husband like a monkey with his long wrinkled upper lip and his bright brown eyes.

'But Madame must go to see the room in which Queen Victoria slept, where she sat of an evening, the view she most admired.'

'Oh, indeed,' cried Charlotte, actually laying down her knife and fork and clapping her hands in excitement at their pleasure, their hold on life; warming herself for a moment at this woman who painted her leathery cheeks a dark crimson out of the very joy of living.

'The waiter,' interposed her brother, 'is trying to attract your attention.'

So she subsided. She ate. Merely commenting to Marion that surely they should visit the castle on the donkeys. The music rose to a little frenzy and it too subsided, allowing to be audible the grating of chairs as the Prussian officers rose as one man from the table, and the clatter of metal as they stripped the hat stand. The voices too hushed as they strode between the tables, swords rattling, loose greatcoats flapping.

There was some joke between them. They laughed and nudged so that when they came opposite the English party, one of them was propelled suddenly forward, very tall and fair with the blood risen in his brown cheeks. He clicked his heels and bowed deeply. All around the room there was a scarcely audible release of tension, of amusement even. Charlotte distinctly heard a tiny patter of laughter.

Are we mocked? she thought in alarm, glancing towards her brother.

But this little scene had been enacted behind his back, and he was now looking in a bewildered way at the backs of the retreating soldiers. The French family sat watching with surprised gravity. Then Madame leant sideways to Charlotte and said with a smile at once sad and significant, 'She is your daughter, Madame? She is a truly beautiful young girl.'

Ellie? Had the tall young officer bowed to Ellie?

'My niece,' she said, and stared at Ellie, who sat bolt upright, looking ahead as if in a trance.

'Who was he?' asked her mother sharply. 'Have you been speaking to him?'

'Of course not,' said Ellie.

'Had you noticed him before?'

'No.' How she scorned them.

'Then we shall behave as if the foolish incident had never happened,' said Marion, and she lifted her knife and fork with such studied composure that she seemed to mime the action of eating.

But something had happened. The entire room's pleasure and awareness of it could still be felt.

Perhaps it could be said that something else had happened too, for Charlotte, glancing around her at the tolerant smiling faces, had seen, watching them with open amusement, the man who looked like Desmond Fermer seated at the table behind them with his stout wife and tall sons.

The Ascent of Stolzenfels

So they were travelling together; might meet, one supposed, exchange words. The wife's voice as she had called, 'Here, Edward, here,' had been her passport to respectability. Well, so be it. It was of no importance. These thoughts fell like strokes of the brush as Charlotte arranged her hair for bed. Ellie leant out through the open window in her white nightdress.

'Who do you suppose he was?' she asked, drawing back into the room, her voice not quite her own but still a part of the world of the moving lights on the dark river.

'Who?'

'That man who bowed to me.'

'Some soldier.'

'An officer!' Already she defended him against all the world, so that Charlotte felt obscure alarm and turned to look directly at Ellie's self.

'Will he be there tomorrow?' She leant against the window frame hugging her arms against the stomach of her white gown, not sharing her delight but toying with it openly for her own amusement. So that Charlotte withered, faded.

'Probably not.' Her voice, she hoped, sounded a firm indifference, for passionately she hoped he would not. He had mocked them all with his beauty and gallantry; cast them aside for their aging and eating, only singling out Ellie from the universal dismissal. Who now said defiantly out the window, but for the benefit of her aunt, 'I hope he will.'

'Oh, Ellie!'

'Oh, Ellie!' She too mocked and called softly into the dark, 'Oh, Ellie, Ellie, Ellie,' hugging herself in her white gown in an ecstasy.

Charlotte too in just such an ecstasy had strayed out into the garden at Melbury and actually kissed an open peony. Why should she remember that, suddenly now, brushing her hair, wondering what she should say to Ellie, with all the strange clarity of a dream? A full moon had enchanted all colour from the garden. Freed from its bright distractions she had felt intensely all around her the life of plants, which seemed a cold moist persistent thing, gripping and sucking its survival, far more akin, after all, to the moon than the sun. She had felt drawn in among them, had stooped to smell the peony and, feeling its cool vigorous flesh brush her cheek, had pressed lips among the petals and kissed them repeatedly. It astonished her to remember that she had done such a thing, a prey at the time to love of Desmond Fermer, but ignorant entirely of what love might be other than a succession of joys and sorrows expe-

·

27

·

rienced exclusively inside herself. For never once had they been alone in a room together. There had been no intimacies between them other than those of the eyes. Once Desmond Fermer had lifted her down from her horse and they had shared for an instant the simulacrum of an embrace. So astonishing had been the sensation of his strength, so violent her reaction that she still remembered it, but even that less vividly than kissing the peony. She had been quite alone at the time, but the incident was indissolubly linked with him.

Now she fairly battered with the brush. How absurd to remember when over the years her forgetting had been so adept. Such thoughts betrayed when it was her duty to be clear-headed and advise. She sought action. Ellie's petticoat, so recently mended, had trailed its border of lace as they had climbed the stairs. She crossed the room to where it lay on the floor and gathering it up carried it to the oil lamp on the table. There she seated herself and opened her little cedarwood box for needle, cotton, and thimble.

Ellie, hearing her restless movements, half turned back into the room. 'What are you doing?'

'Mending your petticoat.'

'Oh, I'll do that.'

But she would not. It had been fresh this evening and must be worn again. She sewed in silence.

'Talk to me.'

'What about?'

'About when you were young.'

'We have been through all that.'

'Not *all*,' said Ellie. Her voice was suddenly shy. 'Were you ever in love?'

Love! Surely she did not equate that young officer's mocking gallantry with love. Rapidly she whipped the lace to the soft stuff of the lawn with tiny biting stitches. 'I thought I was.' For one must never lie.

.

28

.

'How old were you?' That it seemed was the key to everything.

'Eighteen.'

Ellie gave a little laugh out into the night so that Charlotte defended herself quickly, holding the sewing still in her lap. 'I was too young to know my own mind.' But that was untrue. She had known quite well.

'What happened?'

'Ellie, really!'

'Oh, never mind.'

So that she said defiantly, 'Your mama and papa did not consider it a suitable match. They felt in time it would be sure to make me unhappy.'

'He proposed?' It seemed to surprise her.

'Yes,' said Charlotte with asperity, and bowed to her sewing. 'He spoke not to me of course but to your father.'

'And he said no? That was all? You submitted?' The light voice was intolerably bleak.

'It was not a matter of submitting. Your papa only did what he thought was for the best.'

'But you were in love with him?'

'Oh, Ellie, in love? In love?' And indeed as she repeated the words they seemed quite meaningless, as any word can revert suddenly to mere sound. 'It was twenty years ago,' she pleaded, but so too had it been that afternoon, so unexpectedly on a quayside in Prussia. 'And indeed,' she said, 'perhaps all I really wanted was to be away from Melbury.'

'And they made you go?'

'They did not *make* me go. Your Great-uncle Ransome's housekeeper died and the opportunity came for me to take up a useful life that my old life had well prepared me for.' How measured the words sounded. She seemed to pierce them stitch by stitch and bind them into the work in her hands. So much for her entire lifetime.

·

29

·

'And the man?' asked Ellie awkwardly, but not to be denied.

'Oh,' said Charlotte lightly, 'he was older than I. He needed a wife. The mill was his by then. His father had died that winter. He married within the year. A girl from Peaslake.' There was no more to the tale. The rent was mended. She shook the petticoat roughly on her knee. 'There, it is done.'

'Thank you,' said Ellie.

But she would not have pity or any hand laid on that jarred memory. She rose and carried the lamp into the next room. By the time Ellie followed her she was kneeling upright beside the narrow white bed inaccessible in prayer.

They remained at Coblenz for a week, going out by the day for excursions. Charlotte's fear for her niece, if fear it had been, proved unfounded. The young officer did not reappear and Ellie after all did not care. What had he been but a glass in which she had caught an intoxicating glimpse of new powers? Other such glasses would presently be come by. Yet Charlotte noticed that she had a little withdrawn from their old intimacy. She had been rather silent these last days and tonight had gone directly to bed, leaving her aunt alone in their little salon.

Charlotte to her journal:

Today we made the ascent of Stolzenfels to view the castle. A beautiful autumn day. My donkey was called Hans, and was coaxed along by a small flaxen-haired person who could not be prevailed upon to reveal his name. View magnificent. Castle somewhat disappointing. The Queen's apartments somewhat cramped and tasteless. Through the window the same view.

When she had finished she felt overcome with dissatisfaction. The room was airless and littered with Ellie's clothing which she had not the strength to clear away until morning. She moved her journal closer to the lamp, turned back to the earlier pages concerning the tour and read them with astonishment. That she had written so, but a few weeks previously, with such zest, such freshness. No perfunctory phrase like 'view magnificent' had escaped her pen in those days. Nor had she tried to hide the many little vexations of travelling, believing that her pages with some selection might be helpfully shared with others and that these very incidents from which travellers should most learn are soonest forgotten. The words she had just written seemed as false as they were banal. For she had been beset on these expeditions out of Coblenz by a new vexation she had been careful not to record.

Everywhere they had been they had met the other English family, the handsome father, the stout mother, the two tall sons, who glanced at Ellie and then away again. Even now and then, they nodded and smiled, that cautious oblique smile that can be picked up or cast aside without offence. As if by mutual consent, no word was spoken, for then there must be another word and another and of what would they consist? The prospect was alarming. Yet Charlotte, drawn to these people by bonds she knew did not exist, felt the silence oppressive.

She could not be in a room with them, as in the panelled sitting room at Stolzenfels (graced once by the presence of their own Queen) without being intensely aware of them. The younger son, she noticed, hovered by the mother, the elder strove to be in all things like the father. Did they talk among themselves? Did they laugh? Did they love one another? These things she found concerned her. The thought tormented her that this concern might in some way press itself upon them, and noticeably intrude, for the two parties seemed unable to avoid one another.

Yet to avoid them had become Charlotte's most ardent

wish. It seemed the face that had so pained her by its first revelation now haunted her. Glancing up from her Red Guide, directed by Ellie to look over there at this or that, there would be the heavy features, shaped on strong bones, smiling or solemn, the thick fall of dark hair, silvering by the ears. It was almost as if she had caught him staring at her. But that of course was impossible. She was not a woman at whom men stared, having never desired them to do so, and it was after all in her imagination that the bond lay, not in his.

It must therefore be that she was staring at him. That without her willing or controlling it, she turned towards him in her loneliness as a plant will move to face the sun. A stranger, a man of whose soul she wanted nothing, subjected to the constant groping of her eyes. The indecency of it appalled her, and the shame; for soon he must become aware of what was happening, embarrassed, worse, amused.

At the table d'hôte, at noon, leaning back her head in laughter at some remark of Ellie's, she had found herself again staring directly into his laughing face so that for one instant it was impossible not to believe that they shared the same amusement.

'Does he remind you of anyone?' she had whispered to Marion as they had stood fanning themselves with their guidebooks, waiting in this afternoon warmth for their donkeys to arrive and bear them down from Stolzenfels.

'Who? That man?'

He stood alone staring down to where the river shone, broad and motionless in the veiled sun. He had taken a pipe from his pocket and was puffing at it in the German manner. The elder boy lounged against the wall a little way away, with him but respecting his solitude; the younger hovered about his mother, who, red-faced and broad, sat resting on a bench.

'No?' She was questioning Charlotte, who wished now

.

.

that she had not embarked on this but felt compelled to go on.

'Desmond Fermer—from Netherton.' There had been a time when she would have plotted to bring that name into the conversation, so that like a struck match he would exist, flare suddenly in the empty rooms. Now she brought out the words casually enough. 'The mill owner at Netherton? Imagine thinking of him after all these years. I have no recollection of what he looked like.' Marion glanced over her guidebook at the solitary Englishman. 'I doubt I met him more than once or twice.' For he had been supposed beneath them. Nevertheless there had been an anxious flicker in her eye. That name had not passed between them for so long that neither of them could be sure which of its associations they admitted to. So she chose to play at total ignorance. Better perhaps. It had been folly to mention it. Charlotte returned to her prey.

There is little love between them, she thought, as the donkey bells approached. The next batch of tourists was arriving at the head of the path, freeing their mounts for the descent. He was by nature an energetic man, impatient. Charlotte the watcher knew. The wife lethargic, withdrawn, a little sad. The satellite sons anxious between them. They seemed accompanied by an air of unhappiness and disturbance which Charlotte, however inexcusably she pried after their secrets, could not confirm.

Perhaps she was mistaken. Perhaps these speculations were based on nothing more substantial than the quality of his smile which affected one side of his mouth more than the other and considerably narrowed his eyes. It seemed prompted not by any innocent mirth, but an awareness of discrepancy between things as they were generally held to be and as he perceived them.

It was a relief that the days were passing. That when they left Coblenz only two more stops remained on their

·

·

itinerary. There had been enough of this. She was worn down by it. She closed her journal and blew out the lamp. It was possible to make her way to her bedside in the dark for even during this brief stay the rooms had become familiar and taken on a kind of permanence in her thoughts, so that it was difficult to imagine in two nights' time that they would stay in yet another room.

When she had prayed she lay straight and patient in the bed, waiting for sleep. She savoured this borderland between waking and sleeping when the thoughts, still kept under some control, become wayward and eager to take their own course. Often she enjoyed in these moments dreamlike imaginings in which disaster struck at Marion or Ellie, and she, Charlotte the rescuer, preserved them. Then warmed by their gratitude, she passed imperceptibly to sleep.

Now she lay still in the darkened room trying to distinguish from Ellie's light breathing whether she slept or whether she too lay quietly thinking, when her mind filled with an image of Marion lying unconscious on the terrace below the castle at Stolzenfels. She, Charlotte, knelt by her side, first sliding her own folded shawl under her head to protect it from the gravel, then carefully drawing the little crystal bottle of smelling salts that had been her mother's to and fro in front of Marion's rigid face.

The English family bent over her. She explained looking up at them, 'I am her sister-in-law. She has fainted.' Their mouths moved sympathetically, but they made no sound, Charlotte being at a loss as to what they might say. Only the wife seemed to murmur, 'Oh, dear, oh, poor dear,' in a gentle persistent voice. Charlotte was aware of that shock; that sensation of physically falling that sometimes accompanies the onset of sleep, and at the same instant she heard a loud deep masculine voice pronounce as clearly as if someone had entered the room, 'There's no need to fuss.

·

34

·

She's only shamming to get a reaction out of you.' What an odd dream, she thought when it recurred to her in the morning, and immediately put it out of her mind.

At noon, at the table d'hôte, she glanced covertly at the English family's usual place. They were missing, and again in the evening. She told herself of her relief. But during the rest of their stay at Coblenz she felt a depression of spirits, a quickened sense of loss as if ghosts could haunt with their absence as much as by their presence.

The Arrival at Bonn

On the Thursday they took the steamer to Bonn. After breakfast they went down to the pier where they had arrived and there briefly separated. Ellie and Marion boarded the steamer. Mr Morrison went to buy the tickets and to pay off the *laquais de place*. Charlotte was left by the luggage on the crowded pier, counting and recounting in one of the agonies of uncertainty that overcame her when she must change her abode. There were ten pieces and she had counted ten. The responsibility of being left with the luggage when it lay vulnerably on the stones—a part, it seemed, of no life in particular, and so easily commandeered by one person quite as well as another—so weighed upon her that to be sure she counted again. Again the answer was ten, but this time she was convinced that she had counted her own portmanteau twice.

She began again, singling out each piece with her eye. The answer was nine. At any moment her brother would return demanding account. She, the careless steward, must render it diminished. Already the heavy net was dangling over the side and the porters making ready to reload it. Should she attempt to stop them, until she had counted more carefully? She stood on tiptoe in the hope of seeing Mr Morrison approach to resume command, but the press of people trying to board the steamer was too dense. She was jostled continuously so that only slowly did she recognise the pressure on her arm as being more personal and demanding.

She turned to face a young man who entreated her earnestly in German. Only generally by his youth and foreign uniform did she recognise him. In the hotel among his fellow officers he had seemed to threaten. Now he was quite alone. The quick suspicion that he had mocked them had given him mastery. She had thought him older. Even the impression of a defeating beauty had been mistaken. Light has a clarity in the early morning which it loses during the day. She saw the red collar of his coat unfastened and thrown back carelessly to his shoulder. He was bareheaded. The cropped fair hair became him less than his helmet. The sun sparked on his unshaven chin. His features had not yet hardened, the flushed skin had imperfections. Particularly she was aware of a rash on his neck where the stiff uniform had chafed and the movement of his throat as he strained over the unfamiliar words. For seeing her uncomprehending he had begun again. 'You speak French, Madame?'

She nodded but regretted at once that she had laid herself open to him.

He said awkwardly in French, 'Madame, it is necessary that you tell me where you are going?'

He was so hurried, so agitated. She could not feel

towards him the resentment that she should. Had he slept? Where ought he to be at this time of day? She began, 'What possible concern could it be . . . ?'

'You are not her mother. Her friend perhaps? Her sister?'

He meant to flatter. She said, 'You have no business upsetting her. She is a child.' But what possible weight could this carry when now it seemed that he was little more than a child himself.

His face was strained with the effort to understand, then with an eagerness that alarmed her. 'Only tell me where you are going. Where will you be on Saturday?'

'There is no reason at all why I should. Indeed it would be very wrong of me to do so.' She had, without meaning to, lowered her voice so that now she seemed to plead with him like some fellow conspirator. For what if Ellie and Marion should come out on the deck of the waiting steamer and, idly looking down at the quay, see her caught up in earnest conversation? At any moment her brother might return. With a confused intention of protecting everyone she began to walk hastily back towards the city walls, pressing against the continuous stream of late arrivals. He followed noisily with his boots and his sword. 'It is not wrong. I must see her. Speak with her.' There was an edge of authority in his voice. He seemed to insist out of some natural right. So she hardened.

'We have no way of knowing who you are.'

'But you can see who I am.'

She would not confuse herself by looking back at him. It meant nothing, all that she could see of him. Nothing at all.

'On Saturday,' he was pleading. 'On Saturday I shall introduce myself to her father. Only tell me the name of the hotel where you will be staying on Saturday.'

'I don't know—' for surely a lie was justified when he pressed her so.

'The town then? Bonn still? Or Cologne?'

'Cologne,' she said, bringing her gloved hand to her lips, astonished that she had spoken the word. She added in her own defence, 'But you will never find us.'

'I shall find you, never fear. *Au revoir.*' He snatched up her hand and kissed it; then dropping it abruptly, began to run up the cobbled ramp to the wall. At the gate he turned and waved at the steamer, but Charlotte looking sharply could see no answering wave from the deck.

Now that he had gone she was angry again at him for his importunity; at herself for her foolishness. The luggage would have gone now. At any moment the bell would ring. There would be her absence to account for. She must of course tell Marion what had happened. They must be on their guard. But not now. Oh, I am a coward, she thought, hurrying back to the steamer. Not until they had again a room and a bed. Then she might make her confession of foolishness and they might discuss it calmly and in privacy.

The bookings at the Hotel Bellevue had been made in advance from Coblenz. Now in the foyer while they waited for Charles to hand over the passports, an altercation arose as to how the two sets of rooms should be allocated. Ellie, who should have been the last to state her claim, had said impetuously that she wanted very much to sleep in the room overlooking the river. When her mother replied that she would be consulted in her turn, her eyes had inexplicably filled with tears, as instantly as if in response to some blow. She had stood staring at them, wildly Charlotte thought, with the reproachful tears rolling slowly down her cheeks in full view of any guest who cared to look.

Marion withdrew to where her husband waited for the formalities of arrival to be completed.

While the maid and porter stood curiously by, Ellie continued to shed slow hot tears down a motionless face, until Charlotte could not desist from reaching out to dab at them with her own handkerchief. Ellie flinched and looked aside.

Is it possible, thought Charlotte, that she thinks of him. Perhaps she saw me with him.

Now Marion smoothly approached them, smiling her smile of settlement. It appeared that at Coblenz when she and Charles had had the river side, that they had neither, although they had of course made no mention of it, slept well for the noise. So now if Charlotte would not mind the sacrifice—it was of course for Charles's sake—they would take the town side. 'Do you mind?' Her soft mittened hand rested affectionately on Charlotte's arm. The smile she tilted up towards her was charming. Ellie she ignored.

Once in the room, Ellie drew a chair to the narrow window, and sat there with her arm still half entangled in her flowery shawl staring fixedly in the direction from which they had come. She said not a word and the few remarks Charlotte ventured about which drawers in the chest she might take and the possible time for dinner, fell so awkwardly upon the silence, sounded so banal, so like entreaties for forgiveness when really there was nothing to forgive, that she could not bear to continue but moved restlessly about the room taking things from her portmanteau and stowing them carefully into this strange room as if it were to be her home indefinitely.

When she heard her brother's heavy rapid step go past in the direction of the stairs, she said to the silent room, 'I am going for a talk with your mother.'

In the room across the corridor permanence had already been established. The dressing table had been set out in its

.

40

.

proper order. Marion sat at it, enthroned. Any sign of recent arrival had been tidied away by the hotel maid. There was no suggestion at all that they should ever depart. The room itself was pleasant enough, but airless. The windows were muffled in lace curtains. The clean smell of beeswax and the distressing smell of cigar smoke which haunted these places seemed to Charlotte stifling.

'Will you be comfortable here?' she asked anxiously. 'Are you sure you would not like to change?'

'Quite comfortable—' but as she spoke she slid her fingers delicately across her brow and lifted her eyes slightly. It was a signal between them that a headache threatened.

'Oh, I do hope not,' said Charlotte. 'You have done so well lately.'

'What is it? Is it Ellie?'

Clearly if she were unwell she should not be agitated, but Charlotte, important with the burden of her guilt, was not to be restrained. She closed the door behind her and leaning against it said to Marion's reflected face, 'I have done a very foolish thing.'

'Oh, Charlotte!' She laughed although the laughter instantly brought an expression of pain.

'Really I have.'

'It's Ellie,' Marion said, resting her head on her hand. 'I know it's Ellie.'

'It's that young man.'

There was no questioning whom she meant. 'He has approached her?'

'No, no, he has approached me.'

This time she laughed outright. 'Perhaps, Charlotte, it is you that he is after.'

'No. Of course not.'

'I was not being unkind.'

You were, but this she perceived from a painless distance. Men seldom noticed her. She had little desire for the

.

41

.

consequences of their notice. Her pity for him; for his poor unprotected throat had been of quite another order. 'He wanted to know where we were going.'

'And you told him,' said Marion tucking in her soft chin. 'No doubt he was very plausible.'

'He looked very tired,' said Charlotte. 'Very much in earnest.'

Her sister-in-law gave a little snort and said with precision, 'Fortune hunters most commonly are.'

'But she has no fortune.'

'To them all English girls have fortunes. Don't look so worried. It's a simple matter really. If he appears again Charles will deal with him. Only, Charlotte, my dear, you must restrain your tendency to interfere. It would be so much more satisfactory if we could avoid upsetting Charles.'

'But he came upon me unawares,' protested Charlotte. 'I was so taken aback.' There was to be no forgiveness. Indeed she deserved none.

'Fetch Ellie to me,' said Marion. 'It is only fair we warn her of what she has been laid open to.'

In the interval between leaving the room and returning with Ellie the headache seemed to have taken a silent stride. They could feel its thin electric threat. Marion had moved to a chaise by the window, which was now slightly open. The warm evening air sent the muslin curtains stirring and whispering behind her, as she, with her hair loose and her shapeless lilac wrapper, seemed to have transformed herself into a shadow. One hand shielded her eyes from the light that filtered through the curtains, the other she extended to Ellie, who went cautiously towards her.

'Now, Ellie, dearest, you must not be cross with your mama, nor raise your voice. I speak to you for your own good, and although I have every trust in your modesty, we are exposed to awkward situations when we travel—that someone so young as you can have no knowledge of unless someone of more experience instructs you.' She reached out and gently turned Ellie's chin, so that they faced one another. Her eyes dwelt for a moment with that same expression, half affectionate, half speculating, that Charlotte had observed on their first evening at Coblenz and failed to understand.

She continued. 'There was a foolish incident the other evening. If you have as much sense as I think you have you will have forgotten it already. I only feel that I must raise the subject again to warn you that the same young man has been pestering your aunt and that she in her confusion has told him that we should be staying in Cologne by the end of the week.'

Ellie twisted her head away and cried out in loud, eager anger, 'Why didn't you tell me?'

In the same instant she was made aware that the cry directed at Charlotte had fallen as a blow to her mother, who lay back on the chaise with her eyes shut and her hands to her head.

'Mama,' she said in a frightened voice, 'are you in pain?'

'No amount of pain would stop me saying what I must say.' Her eyelids flickered but did not lift. 'Your father will have to be told, although I dread upsetting him. If at any time this man tries to speak to you again, you simply turn and walk away. If he makes any attempt to detain you, your father must report him to the authorities.'

'Why do you hate him so? He's done nothing wrong.' But her mother had succeeded in drawing the conversation down to a level of whispers, and this plea, which should have sounded grand and plaintive, was merely feeble.

'I have said all that I have the strength to say,' said Marion. 'Perhaps, Charlotte, you will be good enough to ring for the maid.'

.
.

By evening the migraine had intensified. Mr Morrison arranged to sup with his child and his sister in their small salon. They were accustomed to the immediacy of his entrances; the light rapid knock with one hand while the other without waiting turned the handle. Then he was borne through the door by the force of whatever thought was uppermost in his mind.

Tonight his hair and cravat were slightly dishevelled. He seemed to bear the imprint of his wife's pain. Immediately the room was alive with the currents of his restless anxiety. He said rather loudly, 'This is indeed a misfortune. Of course tomorrow's expedition must be abandoned.'

They had planned on the following day to cross the river by steamer to Königswinter and from there to take donkeys to the ruins on the summit of Drachenfels. Now all that seemed uncertain. Over their meal they discussed it in hushed voices, as if even at that distance they might disturb the sufferer.

'Have you sent for a doctor?' Charlotte asked.

Apparently the doctor attached to the hotel had a little English. It should not be beyond him to prescribe something to make her better. If only she could sleep. He began to walk agitatedly about the table, trailing his hand on the white cloth. 'She must be got well again by Saturday. On Saturday we are due in Cologne. Is there nothing you can do?' he burst out to Charlotte. 'You must know something that soothes her.'

'Carbonated water,' she said suddenly. 'Don't you remember, Ellie, once she managed to sip some carbonated water and said it soothed her. Shall I send for some?' And she reached towards the bellpull with one of those slightly dramatic gestures that seemed to characterise her efforts to be of use. It was unnecessary. Her brother given a task rushed out of the room. They heard him in the passage calling the maid.

When the meal had been cleared away they withdrew to the bedroom and undressed in silence. Only when they were both in bed did Ellie say softly, 'Why didn't you tell me? What did he say?'

'Oh, Ellie, and your mother made ill by it.'

'Oh, Ellie,' she mocked. 'Oh, Ellie.' She propped herself sideways in the bed on her elbow and whispered eagerly, 'What is his crime? All he has done is to bow. I have flirted with young men before and never lost my heart, if that's what she's afraid of.'

'But not here. Not so far away from home, where quite innocent actions might be misinterpreted.'

'What did he say?' she asked again. 'Did he ask my name?'

'No. He did not.'

'What then? Will he come to Cologne?'

'I think that is what he intends.'

'Oh, how sour you are. What harm is there? It's only an amusement.'

'Then why do you care?'

'I don't care,' she said defiantly. 'I don't care at all.'

After that there was silence until Charlotte whispered, 'Are you awake?'

There was no answer but she sensed an overstillness from Ellie's side of the room that made her suspect that Ellie lay as she did, thinking inconceivable thoughts that would leave no trace on her face when she woke blurred and childish with the passage of sleep. She tried to measure the passage of time that the young officer had appeared before Ellie. Surely not more than a minute. Was it possible to fancy herself in love on the strength of that? There was no possible answer. She was tired.

Now Charlotte walked alone in the shrubbery at Melbury: on close-mown grass between high dark hedges. Although it was dark, the air was dimly luminous: no detail of the green constrained alley in which she moved was hidden. It was quite empty. But in the neighbouring alleys she heard other people moving and talking, she fancied in pairs. Occasionally there was the distinct sound of a skirt brushing the far side of the hedge; once a burst of subdued laughter just by her ear, but when she ran to penetrate the box with her hand, hoping to see through to the other people, she merely released its bitter disconcerting smell. The tight network of leaves and twigs was too dense. She returned to pacing along the damp grass towards the end of the alley.

Because she made no perceptible progress, fear nagged at her that when she reached the end there might be no means of escaping. Nevertheless the box hedge which appeared so solid had sudden gaps, admitting onto different views. Once she saw moving water catching the moonlight. Whether it was brown river or blue sea was impossible to tell. The whole scene was devoid of colour except for a single point where a gentleman stood at the end of the alley overlooking the bright water. His dark shape was outlined against it. The white linen at his neck was clearly visible and the orange tip of a cigar which even at that distance she could see him slowly raise and lower from his lips.

At another place she looked out onto a moonlit lawn. Two girls arm in arm walked back and forth in front of the flower beds. She knew without seeing their faces that they were the Walker girls from the vicarage. They were wrapped in a single pointed shawl, held around both their shoulders. Their wide skirts blended together into a pale blur gliding against the dark foliage. When they stood still it was difficult to distinguish them from the pale heavy clusters of peonies that shone from the edges of the lawn.

Charlotte was no longer alone. A gentleman appeared at her side, saying, 'May I walk with you awhile?'

·

·

With the easy acceptance of dreams Charlotte took his arm and together they walked through the shrubbery. They could hear the other guests rustling deeper in the maze. The Walker girls were laughing. Arm in arm Charlotte and her companion walked steadily towards the man who stood smoking at the end of the alley.

'Do you like to travel?' he asked her.

'Oh, yes. At least I liked it particularly at first. Now I feel discontented. I don't know why. I am ashamed but I do.'

'It is too superficial for you? Perhaps you would like to stay in one place longer.'

'Particularly,' said Charlotte, 'I should like to know what people say.'

'You would find it very dull.'

'Oh, I cannot believe that. Everyone seems to talk to one another with such animation. They seem to have some trick of living.'

'They?' he said. In the dark there was no measuring the intensity with which he watched her. Indeed his face was only generally familiar. 'They? You imply that you have not.'

'You mock me,' she said smiling. 'You can see that I have not.'

'It must be the light. I cannot see that.'

'Even in England I have the greatest difficulty talking to people. I struggle to speak. They answer with effort. Then they move away and a moment later I see them speaking with such animation and intimacy with someone else. It is as if there were whole portions of the language that I have never learned. I long to overhear and learn what words they use.'

'If you should find them just ordinary words as we are using, would you be very disappointed?' He had a deep voice, amused, insinuating. She was not afraid of him.

.

.

'This is not at all an ordinary conversation for me.'

'Nor is it for me.'

She could not sustain the words. Suddenly they deserted her. The shrubbery, the ghostly dresses, the glowing cigar, could not outlive them.

'I am unhappy,' he said, in a last bid for her attention.

'Yes, I know that. I can see that.' But irretrievably he was gone.

An Excursion to Königswinter

At breakfast Mr Morrison informed his daughter and his sister that the night for which so much had been hoped had been a disaster. Students singing and shouting in the streets had kept poor Marion awake until the small hours. When they had tried to shut out the noise, the room had become stifling. Each remembered in silence how the riverside room had been sacrificed to Ellie's whim.

When the doctor had paid a second visit, Charlotte was admitted in whispers to her sister-in-law's room across the corridor. She recognised at once the number of familiar changes that had transformed it into a sickroom. The shutters and curtains were closed. The darkened air was heavy with the scent of eau de cologne, a table drawn up beside the bed was swathed in a white cloth and covered in an array of small bottles and glasses.

Charlotte took her place quietly on a chair by the bedside. Marion's eyes remained closed, the lids and soft skin beneath were smudged with exhaustion. Her faded hair lay over the shoulder of her nightdress in a childish plait. She moved her hand faintly across the surface of the coverlet and Charlotte reached out and took it.

'Are you better, dear, for the medicine?'

With a tiny movement of the head she conveyed that she was not.

'Then we shall cancel the expedition.'

Marion found strength to open her eyes and whisper hoarsely, 'Charles must not be denied his expedition. And you must go with him, Charlotte. He does not like to be without a companion.'

'But Ellie can accompany him.'

The weak voice could still be emphatic. 'Ellie stays with me.'

'But why cannot I stay?' Charlotte persisted in such earnest that without releasing Marion's hand, she slid onto her knees beside the bed. 'I should so like to stay with you.'

This jarring movement served to provoke an expression of pain and the remark, 'Ellie and I are well able to look after one another.'

There was nothing to do but rise to her feet and go. She set aside the hurt of her dismissal and instead, as she softly closed the door, found herself thinking of the cruel invader of her dream who had accused poor Marion of shamming. What does he know of suffering, she thought with indignation, and went to tell her brother what had been decided for them.

So it was that Charlotte found herself on one of the benches on the saloon roof of the ferry taking them over the river to Königswinter. The bell jangled. Steam roared in the miniature tunnel and sent up an angry white plume against the blue sky. The paddles whirled in the noisy water. The whole world was set in motion. Walls, houses, espaliered linden trees, strung out hand in hand along the river front, all withdrew. As did people whose only purpose seemed to be seated on benches staring in front of them, their sluggish interest caught by anything that moved on the river. Presumably they saw Charlotte drawn past them, with as little knowledge as she saw them, thinking, if at all, in words she could never comprehend. She waved her hand to them, but so far as she could see none of them waved back. They dwindled and became obscure. The frail filaments connecting her to them snapped. So Ellie's soldier had watched their steamer and seen it lost. What was left to drag him after her? There had been no cause for fear.

So she swung with the current and watched the complexities of the town slide from her. She felt happy. The miniature boat; the miniature town just visible on the farther bank seemed within control. The excursion had shrunk to manageable proportions. Even their luggage was reduced to her reticule and the black velvet bag in which her brother carried his tracts.

Was he, too, relieved? She glanced from under the fringe of her parasol at Mr Morrison, who sat forward on the bench with his black boots set apart on the deck. His hands were clasped, as if prayer might at any moment overtake him, his face set in lines habitual to him of serious, painful thought. Suddenly he burst out without lowering his powerful voice, 'I should not have left her.'

People turned, startled before they had time to be curious, so that Charlotte answered with elaborate quiet, 'But she wanted you to go. There was nothing else that you could do.'

He began again at his original pitch. 'It was very wrong of me to take you from her.'

'Oh, she did not want me.'

'It is easy to persuade oneself of that,' said her brother, beginning to recover himself, 'when a duty is irksome.'

That was unfair. All in a moment she felt exposed on the bright deck and longed for the absorption and intimacy of the darkened sickroom, from which she now saw her dismissal as the reproach for which it was intended. She had been careless of Ellie.

'And Ellen,' he went on. 'Perhaps she should not see her mother in pain.'

'She has before,' said Charlotte. Sometimes she took these small revenges.

He groaned and shook his head. He had the same enlarged gestures she disliked in herself. In him how readily she forgave. She said with sudden tenderness, 'I'm sure her pain will have run its course by now and she will be sleeping peacefully.'

'It was a mistake,' he replied, 'ever to have come.'

'But the purpose was to restore Marion's health and that surely is greatly improved.'

'Until this last setback. What can have caused that? Unless it is a dread of returning to the life to which I have committed her.' That was his fear. His head slumped forward. He caught it in his hands, deeply dividing the thick grey hair with his fingers. His grief for the moment was absolute.

'But that is not it at all,' she said quickly, 'it is Ellie. Did she not tell you?'

His alarm merely veered. 'Ellie? What of Ellie? Is *she* not well?' He seemed confronted with an epidemic.

'The young soldier at the hotel in Coblenz. Do you remember? He approached me yesterday as we were leaving. He wanted to know where we were going.'

'But Ellen is only a child!'

Between the rails with their thick glistening paint she saw the rapid purpose of brown water. Its strength was frightening. She said, 'She is older than I was when you took me to that dance at Melbury.'

'How odd that you should mention that.' He was silent for a moment with the effort she supposed of remembering her. Then he said, 'You were just a little girl.'

'I was fifteen. I did not feel a little girl. Do you remember my shoes and how displeased Mrs Walker was with me?'

'No.' He laughed, for in a general way he remembered the dance at which he had met his wife. 'I think very little of the past. It is wrong to dwell upon it.'

'But it is a pleasure,' she said quickly, lest he elude her. 'Besides I do not often. Only last night I dreamt of the shrubbery at Melbury.'

He smiled slightly for it was there that in the following summer he had asked Marion to marry him. 'It was always a favourite spot of yours.'

'No, it was not,' she protested. 'I did not like it. It had a strange bitter smell and seemed a place for other people's secrets.' When he said nothing she went on. 'The smell was in the dream and the sounds it made. There was a man smoking a cigar.'

'Marion's father smoked in the shrubbery.'

'It was so real. More like a conscious recollection than a dream. Yet I am sure that if I had set about to recollect, I could not have done so with such clarity. I could not have remembered Mr Weston's cigars. But I promise you I seldom think of it.'

For a moment the landscape had shrunk to the area of her skirt, the slight promontories of her knees, her folded hands, the rough cloth of his trouser leg. His own brown hands moved impulsively to grip hers. 'My poor Charlotte,' he said. 'We were wrong ever to send you away.'

'But you did not send me away. I wanted to go.'

'And now you are back with us.' He spoke with that briskness of someone whose attention has imperceptibly moved in a new direction. His hand surrendered hers for the black velvet bag. For the deck was crowded with people and with his particular sensibility he had felt a moment when the one shore having lost its power over their interest, the other had not entirely claimed it. They moved uneasily in clusters as the tiny steamer swung in the current as if uncertain to which railing to adhere. It was the moment to circulate the tracts. He stood, but when she attempted to rise as well, he said, 'No. I shall manage. You rest.'

It was in her quick sensation of relief that she knew her weakness. There was nothing in his creed she did not cherish except this indiscriminate ministry of it. It was here that she floundered. The slightest movement of her eye took in such numbers. Each unknown. Each with a soul as clamorous and beloved as her own. There was no limit to it. Only their various powers to resist him could give his mission any shape at all. Yet the hurts and humiliations of such resistance were the things she most feared for him. She watched for a moment his tall black form move in among them, vulnerable in his earnestness and excellence. She could not protect him. She could not watch. She went instead to the rail and stood staring down at the water. It swirled now around the paddles as the steamer pivoted and held for a moment against the river's sweep to the sea as if it might succeed in turning and fighting its way back to the source. Then it became apparent that it could do no more than reach the opposite shore which now advanced, extending what it had to offer in the way of more villas, walls, trees, summerhouses.

Mr Morrison returned and took his position beside her once more.

'Were you successful?' she asked him. Successful or not the action had restored and invigorated him.

'They were perhaps a little distracted by the scenery,' he told her. 'But few tracts were dropped and many may be taken out and glanced at later. One little seed to take root is all that is needed, and the beauty of the surroundings can only make them more susceptible to the word of God.'

Green mountains hovered above the approaching town. Now the crowd had clustered at the far rail craning their necks and extending their arms in gestures that seemed to lay claim as much as to identify. Charlotte watched a stout gentleman stride up and down the brief deck with his glass to his eye and swell with importance as he acquired the landscape. She heard exclamations from ladies at the rail laying similar claims to awareness of the beauty that confronted them. The ribbons of their bonnets and the white folds of their panoramic maps fluttered behind them. Loudly their English voices named the hills. But the hills eluded them, slipping behind one another, altering shape, assuming disguises, keeping their mysteries. Carefully schooled in what she should see and feel, Charlotte found herself, with no Marion to prompt, feeling nothing.

This emptiness of spirit seemed lately to have been lowered over her head. She saw but she did not react: saw a black castle at the crease of a hill, a wild dark fleece of forest on one side, neat combed vineyards on the other: knew from the panoramic map its name; knew from *Murray* its dimensions and its particular legend of blood and love and inhuman sacrifice; knew from dutiful reading the previous winter what she should feel—felt not at all.

What has become of me, she thought, I no longer care.

.

.

Since she had recognised the emptiness, indeed the dishonesty of her last entry after the ascent of Stolzenfels, she had not even written in her journal.

Wooden summerhouses perched overhanging garden walls and their wavering reflections. The steep town piled upwards. Above were the strong green hills. To no avail. The brass bell jangled. The boat shuddered against the landing stage. She waited to feel, but felt nothing.

In their turn they disembarked and still arm in arm climbed the steep cobbled street to the donkey station.

As they approached they heard raised voices. The line of donkeys stood patiently waiting, their red harnesses bright against their grey necks. Their dumpy knock-kneed legs seemed forced into dapper hooves a size too small. Each one but the last carried a rider. A knot of tourists stood beside them, some speaking heatedly in a variety of tongues. Between the two groups the donkey boys held apart their hands in gestures of determined helplessness. As Charlotte approached, a boy ran towards her with one finger lifted dramatically skyward. 'One more, one more,' he shouted. Charlotte looked anxiously about her. Surely the people waiting had been there before her.

'We are two,' she said, holding up her fingers and speaking with an exaggerated clarity, 'we are two. One. Two.'

But he was running back to the donkey. 'Madame, Madame,' he called, lifting the stirrup and extending it towards her. 'Come, Madame.'

Suddenly the position became clear. The donkey boys would not set out until every available mount was taken. The tourists, it appeared, came in pairs and did not wish to be separated. Brother and sister said simultaneously:

'I can easily wait.'

'I shall walk.'

A lady turned and, lifting her veil, said pleasantly in English, 'Won't you take my son's donkey, sir,' indicating the youth in advance of her; 'he is young and would enjoy the walk.'

Here then was feeling: the inward jolt: the sudden cessation of sound and motion. Very slowly it seemed to Charlotte, she recognised the Englishwoman mounted behind the younger of her two sons: the wife of the man who looked like Desmond Fermer. She looked up the line of waiting donkeys and riders and there at its head saw the broad back of the father with the taller boy in attendance.

She had supposed them gone, moving ahead of her at such a consistent rate that the misfortune of seeing them on the landing stage at Coblenz need never be repeated. Now it seemed they had only pretended: had gone but a little way only to jump out again like jack-in-the-box, and destroy her peace of mind. But that of course was unreasonable. They were innocent. They meant no harm. The trick of light and shadow on the upstairs landing that terrifies, means no malice. One brings one's fears up the stairs to meet it. The shadow is after all the shadow. The light is only the light.

Now, as he turned, hearing his wife's voice, the shock of his set of features had lessened. The likeness was not really so great as she had supposed. There only remained the embarrassment that, seeing his face, she must endure any sensation on the hidden surfaces of her skin. That it might prove difficult to deal entirely as a stranger, when stranger she was. That most intolerable of all, some heightening or lowering of colour had betrayed her as feeling when she should not feel.

Mr Morrison had gone right up to the lady and, resting one hand on the rough grey neck of her donkey, said, 'Thank you, but I am accustomed to walking and have sorely missed the opportunity for doing so.' The deep weathering of his features, the mildly prophetic cast of his eye were so fitting to his cloth that he never failed to impress. The young man in the act of dismounting, hesitated.

'My sister will take the remaining donkey,' declared Mr Morrison, and with a courteous nod to the lady returned to Charlotte.

She said impulsively, 'Oh, let me walk with you,' and realised when she had spoken that, more than anything, she would like to climb the mountain with him as years ago she had followed him on his visits to the outlying farms of the parish.

He smiled and shook his head. Clearly it was her duty to release the train by mounting the last donkey, and his to insist that she did, but for a moment she was desolated. She thought, He does not wish me with him. I was always a burden upon him and shall be yet.

Obedient as a child, she allowed him to help her into the saddle. A subdued cheer went up from the riders and the waiting tourists. The impasse had been resolved: then a louder cheer as Mr Morrison, gravely lifting and waving his black hat, set off ahead of them up the steep track. He climbed with that light springing step which led his flock to recognise him from afar, and knowing how quickly it would bring him to their doors, make rapid preparations.

There was a delay while saddles were adjusted and veils lowered against the insects of the woods. Before the little donkey train had jolted into motion his vigorous black figure could be seen some little way ahead among the slender close-set birches that barred the bluish sides of the distant hills. He moved so unhesitatingly that he must follow a path.

With a great jangling and shouting the train started forward and for a few moments Charlotte distracted herself

.

.

with the pretence of managing and encouraging her donkey. Then when they had settled to an even patter of sound, and conversation between other tourists had died away, she heard in the distance her brother's fine practised tenor raised without restraint in one of his favourite and most uncompromising hymns. She watched him climb rapidly upwards released from her attachment to the slow indifferent donkey.

Others perhaps shared her envy. One of the boys pointed upwards and his father turned back towards his wife with the odd wolfish smile she had noticed on Stolzenfels. His wife raised her hand to him and a moment later turned and smiled at Charlotte remotely through her veil. It seemed that approval had been relayed down the line to her, and with caution Charlotte returned the smile. Inevitably at some point they must meet and speak. She was glad for this interval in which to dismantle the fantasies she had built about them and make room for the intrusion which must come of their own identities.

The air was warm and smelt of pine. Insects battered the stiff brim of her hat and blundered into her veil. The odour of donkeys rose from their dusty flanks. From the moist floor of the wood came the cool scent of slow decay. As they climbed, the distances simplified and fell away. From time to time Mr Morrison appeared among the trees ahead of them. Then abruptly they saw him no more.

For a time Charlotte was disposed to be anxious, but memories of the past, the fatigues and anxious joys of accompanying him on his parish rounds when he was poor and single, were strongly with her. The woods then had smelt as these did. The white graceful birches, shining among the vivid moss and pale lichen of other tree trunks seemed transported out of childhood. She remembered how, as a young and ardent man, he had often stopped for prayer. Now as then he would have paused at some sight or sound and sunk abruptly to his knees in the presence of his Lord, while she, a child still, awed and frightened that she could not feel the presence of that Male Companion so apparent to him, would play at a little distance; gathering violets, constructing tortuous paths in the pine needles, heaping little dwellings, but never so absorbed as he, frequently looking up to see him, black, rapt motionless, utterly divided from her.

On the Summit at Drachenfels

Nevertheless on arrival she looked eagerly about in the hopes that he might already be there. With a sudden clatter of hoofs the donkey train had left the soft woodland path and come out on to bare rock. They halted near the summit. Above them rose the black perpendicular crag that lifted up the castle like a final excrescence of itself. Ahead on a narrow plateau was a small guest house and scattered among the trees on its natural terrace rustic benches and tables covered with red-and-white checked cloths.

The guide helped her to dismount. He did not smile. She wondered if she should offer him money. Was it expected? She carried none. My brother—should she explain?

My brother will pay you when he arrives. Perhaps he is here already, I must find him. But he had turned his back upon her before she had found the words.

The rest of the party had moved ahead in pairs and little groups: some settling immediately at the scattered tables, others drifting towards the wooden railing that bound the terrace. Below the mountainside must fall steeply away, for the tops of the pine trees just cleared its bars.

Charlotte herself moved slowly towards this railing. She had no desire to overtake the English family whom she could see moving briskly ahead of her as if they had business in this place. Almost immediately they separated. The father strode to a gap in the railing and plunged, it seemed violently, out of sight down an invisible path on the mountainside. She could hear the undergrowth break and snap as he fled the restraints imposed upon him by the ascent. The sons, after a moment's consultation, struck out towards the summit. The wife, left alone again, began to walk slowly and languorously to and fro by the railings, looking sometimes after her husband and sometimes out at the distant prospect, carrying about her that air of contained sadness that made Charlotte fearful of approaching her. Yet it occurred to her that she should, that Marion would expect her to. Careful as one must be there was no question that the Englishwoman was a suitable acquaintance. Her sons might provide a useful distraction for Ellie. If Marion had been there undoubtedly she would have managed it all. But Charlotte held back and going a little to one side braced her arms lightly against the rough red bark of the railing and stared down at the world so revealed to her.

On either side a wild expanse of wooded hills stretched for great distances, mound upon mound, suggestive of giant bone and muscle. Dark shadows stroked them and

.

62

.

passed. Here and there on the steep slope the mat of tree-tops was broken by a road where a peasant woman like a doll pushed a miniature wooden cart and a field where a toy ox-team slowly toiled. Far below, the river like a dull metal ribbon appeared to have halted.

Sounds rose up to her clear and distinct, each with its tale of human activity uninterrupted by any passage of hers. Goats grazed on the grassy shelf below the hotel. Their bells clanked changes. They bleated constantly in shrill coughing voices. There was a little girl who tended them. From some hidden quarry came the clinking of a hundred hammers. A dog barked. A human voice called from a farmhouse whose roof and white smoke were just visible among the trees. For how many days had she stared up at the array of little towns and castles set out along the steep banks of the river. Now raised to this height it seemed that she had been permitted to peer over the top of a painted backdrop.

Perhaps it was the illusion of intimacy and admittance to this complete and miniature world that made her imagine herself the woman whose voice had carried distantly from the farmyard door. She seemed to see herself moving about its unknown rooms, small bare white rooms through which the sun fell at an angle. Here she set a plant on a deep sill. There she hung the sampler she had worked for her mother as a child: her own possessions. All her adult life she had lived in houses built of deep accretions of other people's lives. She had moved among them cautiously. But here, she herself might extend to the very walls and they would reflect back upon her, her plant, her sampler, things that were herself.

Was it a pleasing fancy, or a forbidding one? She scarcely knew. But her thoughts were so concentrated upon it that she failed to notice the Englishwoman's approach.

.

.

Then a slight giving of the rail on which Charlotte leant caused her to look around and see her standing only a few feet away looking down at the same spreading view. A moment later she turned her head and spoke. 'Your brother is a very strong walker.'

'He has a country parish. He walks the hills almost daily.' Shyness which assailed her in those very moments when she wished to please made her look down at the dusty gravel of the terrace and deadened that animation of voice that invites an answer. People's attention is captured or lost in a moment and she was aware of a sudden vagueness in the Englishwoman's eye, an imperceptible movement away along the rail. She could think of nothing to say to recall her. When she did speak she was perhaps too personal. She said, 'I think he will remember this afternoon with more pleasure than the rest of the summer.'

Surprisingly the woman smiled slightly and said half to herself, 'I know. I should like to walk freely as I do at home. I should like to be at home.'

Immediately she moved away. It was the kind of remark one exchanges with a stranger, and perhaps it condemned Charlotte always to be one. She too turned from the view and took a seat at one of the little tables. A girl with blonde pigtails clattered past in wooden shoes to the railing and called shrilly down, perhaps to the goatherd. Immediately she clattered back again. An older boy, tall and thin and very straight, moved between the tables with bottles caught between the fingers of one hand and glasses between the other. He proffered wine, but she explained that she had no money; that she waited for her brother.

She opened *Murray's Handbook* on the table in front of her and set herself to read those lines of Lord Byron's so conveniently reprinted there to save the necessity of carrying both volumes to the summit.

·

·

The castled crag of Drachenfels
Frowns o'er the wide and winding Rhine . . .

But even as she read the image that haunted her was of empty whitewashed rooms. All the more fearful since Mr Ransome's legacy had forced upon her the possibility of living alone. She read a line or two, then glanced at the opening of the path where at any moment her brother might appear.

In a few moments she saw him emerge. He did not pause to look around him as he came out into the clearing, but as if he knew by prescience exactly where she would be, he made directly towards her with no sign at all of fatigue in his rapid eager gait.

He drew back a chair and sat down without ever taking his eyes from her, saying directly, 'I have had sweet communion with the Lord, concerning, among other matters, you.'

'Oh, yes?' Between them it was clear some decision for her had been made.

'We have not spoken directly about the matter before although it has often been the subject of my most earnest prayers as I am sure it has been of yours, my dear sister—' The sudden formality of this address gave the occasion an air of ritual. 'I mean of course the question of your spending the remainder of your life under our roof. I am now convinced that this is the right, indeed the only, course of action for us all to take.'

Oddly she felt the warm discomfort of tears behind her eyes. It was so what she had wanted. Safe in an instant; inside the shelter his words had erected, her mind released a flock of doubts.

'But I should be a burden to you both.' She stretched her thin arm across the table and caught his wrist in her fingers. 'A terrible intrusion on what privacy you have.'

He covered her hand with his own, releasing her anxious fingers as he did so. 'Of course in any financial sense you will cease to be a burden once old Mr Ransome's will passes through probate.'

Her doubts were of the kind that feed and multiply on any attempt at reason. 'I had not meant that. I meant that my company might be burdensome to you.'

All the authoritative lines in his face gathered into a smile of such warmth, such penetration. 'Your company is very dear to us.'

'But day after day,' she pleaded.

'Life is made up of one day after another. You would not wish to spend it so alone.'

'Oh, I should not!' For he had fingered her deepest fear. 'You have kindly, generously, offered me the thing I most want in all the world, only—'

'Only?'

'Only I should like to hear from Marion's own lips that she desires it too.'

'But you shall, you foolish girl. We have often discussed it and joined in prayer on the subject. We are all in total accord in this, as through God's grace we are in all things.'

'She has said nothing to me.'

'That is because we decided that I was the natural person to speak with you, because of our close bond of affection, and because'—he hesitated here—'because it was I who insisted on your leaving Melbury all those years ago.'

'It was not you. It was she.' The impetus of her words startled them both. 'Besides, I wanted to go.' She had withdrawn her hand. For a portion of a second they stood back from something revealed.

Then he said gently, 'We have agreed not to think of the past.'

He had agreed. He had stated.

.

.

'Believe me, she wants you to come. She is not strong and there are no end of little tasks from which you can release her. If you make your home with us—as I trust you will—you will be of great service to her and spare Ellie much.'

'That is what I have always wanted.'

'My good girl. I knew you should. Your proper home is with us.'

'It is very good of you.'

'It is decided then,' he said happily. 'We need not discuss it more.'

So be it. Why feel a bleakness at this sudden settling of her life, without bells, without flowers, without the sharp patter of rice.

'Well,' he said, rising and holding out his hand, 'won't you climb to the summit with me?'

But she found that she did not want to. Indeed doubted that she could. She smiled and said no; she had fatigued herself with the ride and with standing and staring at the view. Besides, they must move off soon. She would sit a little and rest herself for the descent.

As soon as he was gone, she got to her feet and walked restlessly into the guest house. There she made a show of studying the objects set for sale in glass cases: prints of well-known river views, panoramas of the Rhine, bottles of eau de Cologne. None of them could she bring herself to want. She went outside again and wandered over to the railing. The sun had fallen behind the mountain. It no longer warmed her. She stayed for a few minutes more watching the great landscape fallen silent. A wraith of white mist had appeared along the line of the river. Mist cast a bloom over the green swelling hills. She was cold now. No one, no sound emerged from the path down which the Englishman had disappeared. She turned and went back to the inn, where the tourists had begun to assemble and the line of donkeys waited. It was time to descend.

Already some of the donkeys were mounted. The donkey boys began to call out words that were unintelligible but successfully created an air of urgency. Charles appeared briskly from the summit and joined her. The Englishwoman waited anxiously between her sons, staring now at the donkeys, now at the break in the terrace railings where the path plunged down among the trees. So he had spent the afternoon alone, apart from them. The elder son went in search. Faint halloos were heard and a moment later, with his son at his side, the Englishman emerged through the gap, mopping his brow, shouting an explanation, waving them all to mount. A large French family appeared from another path and gave vent to screams as one of their number discovered that she had trapped inside her veil a bee. Amid sobbing and shouting and flapping she was persuaded into the saddle and instantly they set out down through the swiftly cooling woods. It was the last descent of the day and this time no attempt had been made to wait for mounts for the superfluous donkeys. Most of the day's tourists had gone before. Some of the latecomers had stayed at the inn to watch the sunrise. The deck of the little steamer, when they had safely regained it, was far less crowded. The sudden cooling of the air had driven many of the less hardy into the cabin. On the half-empty deck Charlotte and her brother again encountered the English family and this time entered irrevocably on the perils of acquaintanceship.

After all one may perhaps approach a clergyman of one's own faith more freely than most strangers. Presuming him blameless, one's motives in making his acquaintance can only be the same. And so while the Englishman again moved off restlessly to the rail, his wife came up to Charlotte and Mr Morrison and, after some remark about the

·

·

drop in temperature, simply introduced herself. A moment later her husband joined them, approaching with a vigour of stride out of proportion to the narrow deck and an expression of open interest on his face. The sons hovered and smiled behind their parents' shoulders.

Their name was Newman. How surely and comfortingly people dwindle when they speak. Now drawn into the bounds of formal introduction, Charlotte and Mrs Newman conversed with intense correctness. The awkwardness, the sudden near intimacy of their exchange on the mountaintop was quite put aside.

On hearing of Marion's illness Mrs Newman wondered if there were anything she might do. And as if to reassure Charlotte that she would not presume on so slight an acquaintance to do anything at all, mentioned the name of their hotel in Bonn, which was different from that of the Morrisons'.

But in Cologne, it appeared, after another cautious exchange, they would once more be under the same roof. Charlotte, remembering that they had chosen the Hotel de Cologne, amongst others, for *Murray's* recommendation that it was moderate and quiet, felt that this in itself recommended the same virtues in the Newmans. How strange, they agreed. What a coincidence. She is not really speaking any more than I am, thought Charlotte, yet it pleased her that they both managed so well to do so. Perhaps, she thought, she will be my friend.

In a slow comfortable voice Mrs Newman explained their presence in Germany. Mr Newman it appeared owned a sugar refinery in Liverpool. And here, as he stood slightly smiling as his wife gave account of him, it was surely permissible to look at last directly at his face and read what it might reveal. Eyes direct, intelligent. Mouth resolute but not immobile, affected by the same vigour and restlessness that informed his confined movements about

.

.

the deck and narrow terraces. She liked him well enough, but wondered now that she should ever have mistaken him for Desmond Fermer, when the likeness, if indeed she could in honesty remember at all, was so very superficial. Already Charlotte had reached that stage of knowing the Newmans where her initial image of them—she, as aloof and sad: he, invested by accident with her own long-contained capacity to love—stood aside and apart from their real faces, which now at every word and slight alteration of position built themselves in more and more detail into something quite different. As a young man, Mrs Newman continued placidly, while he stood smiling down at her, her husband had studied his trade in Cologne itself and had there learned the language.

'Surely there was little beyond the language you could profitably learn there,' declared Mr Morrison. 'I should have rather expected a Prussian to visit Liverpool if he wished to observe progress.'

Would he so soon offend? But the answer was a curteous enough contradiction, couched as complete agreement.

'Yes, indeed, the son of the family with whom I stayed returned to England with me, but the benefits were mutual. All forms of administration in this country are carried out with such zeal and efficiency. Their manufactories are still on the whole smaller than ours, but in many ways they are better regulated.'

'But freedom, sir!' demanded Mr Morrison. 'What of freedom?'

Charlotte hastened to ask Mrs Newman if she too spoke German. She spoke a little. The German of the kitchen. She had kept since the early spring an apartment in Heidelberg, which she proceeded to describe in such detail as she might have supposed her interested in taking up the letting. Meanwhile her husband had travelled, rejoining them at Coblenz, and her sons had attended lectures at the university. She intimated that her landlady had been found wanting. Over her account of these domestic matters there brooded that faint air of regret that Charlotte had first sensed when she had watched her seated on the bench at Stolzenfels, and perhaps—or did she imagine it—the subtlest of suggestions that her husband was accountable for this.

It was then that he turned and directed a question towards Charlotte. He held no terrors for her now. She could even see that he was not entirely a gentlemanly person. How does one know other than by a sensibility to the minutest details of dress and speech imbued by years of caution in such matters. Yet she liked the frankness with which he addressed her, as if the little effort to draw her into the conversation should be taken as a matter of course. He asked her if she looked forward to visiting the cathedral at Cologne.

'We do not intend to *visit* the cathedral,' answered Mr Morrison. 'What is of real interest, the progress of the building, will be visible from without. As for what goes on inside, I should scarcely care for my wife and child to be exposed to such an atmosphere of superstition and venial preying upon the ignorant and credulous. When one thinks that these are the very people who are agitating for freedom of conscience! What freedom do they ask but to subject themselves still further to a degrading spiritual bondage?'

Mr Newman had watched the clergyman throughout this impassioned speech. He made no attempt to answer, but returned his look, a little ironically, to Charlotte to whom he had originally addressed his question.

Her brother who was forever a sensitive man noticed this and intervened again. 'Miss Morrison is a member of my household and is advised by me in these matters.'

Mrs Newman said placidly that her main object in visit-

.

71

.

ing Cologne was to purchase a crate of toilet water more economically than she could hope to do at home. The remark successfully released them from one another. They were able to comment all at once on the sudden approach of the Cologne landing stage and say goodbye to one another with no more confusion than a sudden arrival makes quite in order.

At the hotel they found Marion propped upright against her pillows with a faint colour in her cheeks. She declared the pain quite gone with a frail courage that impressed upon them that some of it at least remained. There was no question but that she would travel tomorrow. She questioned Charlotte closely about the Newmans. Charlotte told her in as much detail as she was able. Then taking Marion's hand again she said shyly, 'Charles told me you would both be pleased if I made my home with you. I should so like to.'

For some reason she suddenly lowered her head onto the coverlet and burst into tears. She felt Marion groping to stroke her hair and heard her say sympathetically, 'Poor Charlotte, you must have been exhausted by your outing. You must not let me detain you.'

Ellie was slow going to bed. She sat on a chair by the long window staring out to the river humming softly. She was not disposed to talk, but Charlotte had little doubt as to where her thoughts played. Should she try to protect her from disappointment? To voice her conviction of the morning that the young man was lost; would not follow; would not appear. 'What are you thinking about?' she began when finally Ellie lay in the neighbouring bed.

'Nothing,' said Ellie. Charlotte could see the point of her white shoulder hunched against her dark hair. She had turned away. Charlotte lay on her back staring at the window. The thin white curtains blew into the room like veiling and fell lifeless against the wall. I want to go back, she thought. She tried to rebuild out of memory the garden at Melbury. The long black hands of a cedar had swept over the ground leaving all dead and bare beneath them, except for a thin debris of brown needles and little squarish crimson berries like drops of blood. The pale clumps of peonies had stood against the dark foliage. There had been a shrubbery, but never so high and thick as in her dreams of the previous night. Nor had any stretch of water been visible from its alleys. That she had visited a real place on the night before she never doubted. But where could she have seen it? Perhaps it had been here recently: in one of those steep green spaces lying between the river and some painted villa just glimpsed between the trees. But where? Last night Königswinter had been unknown to them. On the outskirts of Coblenz perhaps, or entering Bonn?

It seemed that to reach it she must climb a path between birch trees. The trees were so closely established that they seemed at times to press in upon her like the bars of a cage. Sometimes she hauled herself up by them, for the path was increasingly steep. Sometimes she had to force her way between them. Just as she thought, I cannot, they yielded and let her through. Her companion of the night before was somewhere ahead of her. She could hear the exaggerated din of his footsteps among the leaves and sticks. He sang as he climbed: a loud student song in German that echoed slightly among the trees.

The singing stopped. She called out, 'Will you wait for me? I am just behind you.' It would be impossible to walk arm in arm with him between the narrow trees, but immediately she stood beside him with her hand warmly folded into the woollen stuff of his coat sleeve. The trees had given way to them. Beyond she was aware of powerful distances that tugged at her attention. She told herself that she must look at his face and make out who he was. But instead she kept turning her head this way and that, searching out the distances that it was quite impossible to see.

Is this happening to me, she thought. Am I making it happen? Could I alter it or make it stop? But she made no attempt to rouse herself. Instinct told her how fragile was her hold on what she saw. Move, open her eyes, and she might squander it all, when most she wanted it.

'Well,' he said. 'What do you want?'

She said stiffly, 'I ask nothing of you.' She would not look at him.

'You ran behind me calling my name.'

'I cannot have done that, I do not know your name.' She tried to withdraw her hand, but this became infinitely difficult to do, as if powerful forces dragged at it from the dark woollen spaces between his elbow and his ribs. 'I have made a mistake. I thought you were someone else.' But as she said that, she knew it to be untrue.

'Goodnight.' At last she had been able to withdraw her hand.

'I'll walk back with you,' he said. 'You should not be alone.'

'You mean I am behaving oddly. Do you imagine I shall throw myself into the river?'

'No, of course not.'

'But that is what you meant.'

There. She had annoyed him. He was sullen now. 'Really, you must not suppose that when I say one thing I mean another. When I am with you I ought to feel free to speak my mind. What you choose to do is up to you.'

'I doubt my thoughts would interest you.'

'Perhaps not.' He stood facing her, looking impatiently down at her with his arm braced against a tree trunk. 'You followed me up here with the purpose of asking me something. Say what it is. Otherwise it will hang between us. Damn it, when you're not like this I enjoy talking with you.'

'You do?' That he should say such a thing astonished her.

'You don't believe me?'

'Would you believe me?' she said eagerly. She was looking at him now. 'Would you believe me that all I want of you is the opportunity to talk occasionally? Nothing more. It seems odd that there is any impropriety in asking that, but of course there is.'

He shrugged. He does not care, thought Charlotte.

'Do you believe me? That I mean you no harm? No wrong?'

'I believe you are incredibly sincere.'

'But very inexperienced?'

'Very.' He laughed shortly, utterly excluding her.

'Does that make me absurd?'

'It makes you frightening. Your intensity frightens me.'

'At least,' she said bitterly, 'I have spoken my mind. You cannot accuse me of not doing that.'

'You were happy enough to let your brother speak it for you earlier.'

'But that was to a stranger.'

He had brought his face very close to hers. When he spoke she actually felt warm breath on her cheek and turned away instinctively for gentlemen's breath is often unpleasant, but his was not. His face seemed to follow her like a moon, oddly blurred, by his emotion or by hers, who could distinguish? His breath was warm, sweet, and compelling; his voice private and plaintive. 'But I am not a stranger. Surely not entirely a stranger.'

But she protested then: 'No, no, no.'

SEVEN

A Passage to Cologne

The following morning they took their final passage by steamer to Cologne.

No sooner was Marion settled in the cabin than she said to Charlotte, 'I do not see your friends the Newmans.'

'They are scarcely friends,' said Charlotte, affecting to look about her although she had known the moment she entered the cabin that they were not there.

'Well then, we must exert ourselves and make them at least acquaintances. For Ellie's sake,' she added in a significant whisper. Clearly she too hoped that the sons might provide a distraction.

'But we know nothing of them.'

'We know a little. They are at least English. Oh, Charlotte, I am not suggesting a lifelong friendship. They will be easy enough to shake off after a day or two. But just at the moment we might be glad of their company. Might they be on deck?'

'If they are on the steamer at all,' said Charlotte unaccountably, for she had seen them ahead on the gangplank but judged herself far enough away to be thought not to have done.

'Then shall we take a turn about the deck?'

'But you are not well enough!'

'Nonsense. Fresh air will do me good. Come, Ellie.'

Seeing Charlotte make no move, she said impatiently, 'Well?'

'I should keep the seats,' said Charlotte.

'But it is you who must introduce us.'

For a moment it seemed to Charlotte that she must refuse; that any further contact with the Newmans was simply intolerable. Had there been any hope of saying no, without being pressed for an explanation, she would have refused outright. But what explanation could there be? Could she tell Marion that she was the victim of an immodest fantasy? Of her intrusions upon the mind of a stranger and the sanctity of his marriage. 'Oh, you are excessive,' she cried to herself, climbing the narrow companionway behind her sister-in-law. 'You have done nothing.' Yet he who thinks adultery has committed it. But she was not unreasonable, nor after a lifetime of parish work was she ignorant. The approach to a kiss within a dream was measurably remote from any fact of adultery: an act so encumbered with deceit and strange rooms and the removal of clothing as to be surely almost unmanageable. Her trespass was invisible. There were no footsteps discernible in the dew. No one could know.

And so it seemed to her, when almost immediately after they came on deck they encountered the Newmans that she was indeed an invisible presence among them. She made the necessary introductions and it seemed that man, wife, and sons, their eyes slid over her and fastened upon Marion and Ellie. Of course, she thought, it was they all along that Mrs Newman wished to meet. And he is indifferent.

He hovered for a moment until groups were formed: Marion, Mrs Newman, and Charlotte; Ellie shyly flanked by the two sons. Then he took his stance at the rail again while they strolled on the sunny morning deck in the narrow passage left by the pile of luggage heaped around the foremast.

So far her fears were groundless. Nothing shows, she said to herself, nothing shows. There was little need to make conversation as Marion and Mrs Newman appeared to take an instant liking to one another. The talk traversed the same ground as on the day before: the vagaries of hotels, purchases, the silently borne fatigues of travel, but it seemed to Charlotte that they spoke together with far more conviction and interest than she had managed. How they agreed. How they seemed to gather strength from their agreement from one another for future ordeals. Quite vanished from Mrs Newman was that glint of individual unhappiness that Charlotte had imagined she had seen on the mountaintop and fancied she might befriend. She could see her now as quite another woman, as Marion's new friend joined with her in the universal flow of womanly suffering. She seemed to have a different face and a different voice. And perhaps, she thought a little wildly, watching the French and English tourists as they passed and repassed on their promenade, I could take any one of them and turn them into an inhabitant of the mind. So that they would walk past outside me and inside me be a different person with a different face, different thoughts. She felt unhappy and confused. When they passed Mr

·

·

Newman, sometimes he turned and smiled his disconcerting irregular smile, sometimes he continued to lean over the rail all unaware of them. Then, when they passed him next, he was shouting and pointing ahead.

'It must be the Domkirche already,' said Marion, visibly preparing herself for new and complex reactions. But he was not pointing to the shore, and the watchers for the cathedral spires all at once abandoned their vantage points and surged to the opposite rail. English voices repeated, 'Oh, it's a barge. Look, a barge.' From ahead they heard the sound of men's voices singing.

When they joined Mr Newman at the rail they could see that they were overtaking one of the remarkable log rafts of which they had read in detail.

'Oh, my *Murray*,' cried Marion. 'Don't say I am without my *Murray*.'

'But look at it, Mama,' cried Ellie. 'Don't start reading about it or you will miss it altogether.'

Indeed they were actually overtaking it. 'Oh, the good fortune,' Marion cried, 'actually to see one. It was my dearest wish,' she said, taking her new friend's arm as they pressed upon the rail.

Here was distraction. Another world.

First they overtook the small boats being drawn after the raft, then the line of men with their long oars stretching up over their heads; turning their faces, breaking their singing to shout unknown words which could be friendly or mocking. Impossible to tell which. From the wooden bridge the captain and the pilot gravely waved. Then slowly there drew past a floating village fascinating in its detail and completeness. So that they cried out to one another over the most ordinary things: the ranks of pots and pans visible in a wooden kitchen hut, the haunch of beef hanging outside. Glass in the window of what must be the captain's hut and—oh, look, a plant in a pot. All of

79

them made quite extraordinary by their circumstances. And now a dog ran barking over the platform of chained logs and a small boy ran after him. There was no rail. 'I should never have a moment's peace,' said Marion the mother to Mrs Newman the mother. Oh, the danger! But as if by long instinct they drew up just at the very edge of the platform and stood there perilously looking up at the passing steamer. So near the edge so flat to the water that the boy's bare toes seemed to touch his reflected toes and the dog's forepaws poise braced on his reflected paws. Down into the clear still water the rest of their beings wavered, so that Charlotte watched in a kind of breathless dread for the moment when the agitation of the steamer's paddles would disrupt those images.

She did not see what happened. Afterwards as the events of that day were discussed again she tried to recall those particular moments. The barking dog with its head tossing this way and that. The child with its shock of fair hair. Then a confused movement near her at the rail. Shouts on the deck. How slowly the mind responds to what it has not already imagined. A woman's voice near her screamed. Still she was staring at the boy and the dog being drawn slowly past her. And recognised that Mrs Newman had screamed and that some event was taking place not on the raft but on the deck behind her. And turned. And saw the frightened bands of tourists part and huddle, leaving a space by the opposite rail towards which Mr Newman, inexplicably in his shirt sleeves, ran, and over which as if in some preposterous dream he climbed and vanished. The gap on the far rail closed with a hushed crowd staring down. Mrs Newman screamed again. People near to them drew back. It was apparent that she had fallen. A respectful place cleared around her. Marion's peremptory voice called, 'Salts, Charlotte, salts!'

Automatically she groped in her reticule and reaching

forward handed the little bottle to Marion, who knelt on the deck cradling Mrs Newman's twisted head in her lap. All she could think was, He has killed himself. For some reason he has killed himself. Ellie stood over her mother white and frightened. One of the Newman boys had run to the opposite side. The other had run forward. The paddles had shuddered to a halt. People were shouting again and it penetrated Charlotte's shocked awareness that people do not shout so when they watch a drowning but when they partake of a hunt.

Someone shouted, 'He's alive! He'll get him yet!' A cheer went up. The younger son forcing his way through the crowd that had elected to watch the minor drama of the fainting woman, knelt at his mother's side and repeated, 'He's all right, Mother, he's all right.' She, jerking her head from the painful fumes of the little bottle, muttered, 'Edward, Edward.'

The boy said again, 'He's all right, Mother. He's all right.' Until finally her eyes widened a moment in comprehension and then closed again. It was decided to carry her below to the cabin. A way was cleared. A gentleman stepped forward and carefully lifted her. 'The poor soul. Oh, the poor lady,' rippled among the crowd of watchers like a litany. The boy stayed beside her carrying the bag and shawl that she had dropped. Marion and Ellie followed. And should she go with them? But she was not wanted. Not needed in the least. Nor was she, as Marion had been, primarily concerned with Mrs Newman. She began to make her way forward, straining to see what had happened.

So shaken were her thoughts that it astonished her to find the log platform still beside them. Time seemed to have undergone some strange delay. As she pushed her way along, her mind worried after logical explanations as if this alone were important. They had been overtaking the raft, but then it was so long. The engines had been cut, so now

.

.

perhaps they drifted at the river's pace together. The men at the prow of the steamer hastened now to the raft side. A shout went up, 'Is he dead?,' and it seemed that all around her the word was repeated and repeated as senselessly as by an echo.

She began to push among them asking everyone she touched, 'Is he dead? Tell me what has happened.'

Finally someone without looking at her said, 'Not our man, but the other looks dead enough.' But still she could not be sure.

Then her arm was taken from behind and she was turned to face her brother. He said angrily, 'What are you doing? Why are you here? Why are you not with Mrs Newman?'

'What has happened?' she said. 'Is he dead?'

'I shall take you below.'

'But what has happened?'

Still holding her arm it appeared that he could not resist looking with her over the side. Now the people on the raft could be observed running and gathering in a cluster at a point a little ahead of them. They saw a man roll a barrel across the log floor. A man from the raft jumped into one of the small towed boats and drifted the short interval to the steamer. There, using his oars to keep stationary, he shouted up some request in German.

A voice on the deck called out, 'Is there a priest on board? A man is dying.'

'But which man?' she cried to her brother. 'Which man is dying?'

Mr Morrison shouted, 'I am a celebrant of the Church of England, but no priest. Is the man Catholic or Protestant?'

Shouts were exchanged. 'Hurry,' called the interpreter on the deck. 'He doesn't know, but hurry.' He could be seen stretching his head above the others searching for the man to whom he spoke.

'I am coming,' called Mr Morrison. The crowd shrank back from him. Charlotte was left holding his arm in the centre of a ring of eager expectant faces looking forward now to a prolongation of the drama. Immediately her mind cleared. She said, 'You must not go.'

He laid his hand over hers, cold, shaking. It was intolerable that he was afraid, that his eyes appealed directly to her, but for what? He said, 'A soul is in jeopardy. I have no choice but to go.'

'But perhaps he is already dead.' A sailor heaped a coiled rope ladder onto the rail and threw it over. She heard it rattle down the side of the steamer. Now the crowd seemed to propel Charles towards it, by patting him on the shoulder and so pushing him forward, by reaching to seize his hand and so pull him from her. There was an air of hushed emotion. She saw a man weep and thought, oh, surely that is excessive. Still she clung to his arm and tightened her grip on the black cloth as they reached the top of the rope ladder. But he pulled his hand away, saying, 'Go to Marion. Oh, for God's sake, go to Marion.' Now she was pushed back. His pale alarmed face vanished from her as they helped him over the side. She was convinced that he was being delivered to his death, on that swift current, that perilous raft. She could not go to Marion. What could she say to her?

There was a shout from below. She supposed that he must at least have safely descended to the boat. Already the eager spectators had pushed her back from the rail. She began to work her way forward again, until she could look down and be sure that the narrow channel was safely crossed and see her brother's black figure being hauled aboard the log raft.

There in the space made for him she saw the barrel with the limp form of a man laid over it. As Mr Morrison approached they lifted the body down and laid it on the deal planks. Even at that distance, the gentleness and awe of their movements conveyed itself, as did the senseless pressure of the man's face against the planks.

She saw then the same little boy lifted up on a young man's shoulder so that he might see death, as one might lift a child to see a passing monarch.

For a long time her brother knelt praying after the departed soul. When he raised his head they helped him to his feet and lifting the body with the same fearful gentleness carried it into one of the huts on the raft. It was then that she saw Edward Newman standing a little to one side with a grey blanket thrown over his head and shoulders and clutched under his chin. He stood a little to one side and for a second she could not free her mind of the thought that he looked like a visitant at his own obsequies. Then she told herself firmly that he was alive. She had seen him with her own eyes. It was someone else who had drowned.

Charlotte made her way down to the cabin. She felt weak and shaken and constantly reached out to support herself on any rail or handle she could see. No one attempted to help her for which she was grateful. She was filled with anxiety now for Marion and remorse that she had not gone directly to console her as Charles had urged in what, it still seemed evident, might have been his last words to her. She felt very close to tears, but was acutely aware that she was among strangers and having no designated role as wife or child to any of the leading characters in the tragedy, had no right publicly to give way to feeling.

On entering the cabin she found Marion and Mrs Newman in each other's arms weeping legitimately. A cluster of solicitous ladies was grouped around them like figures in a *tableau vivant*. 'Oh, Charlotte,' Marion cried, stretching out a free arm to her, 'where have you been?'

She came directly and knelt by her, embarrassed by the

close proximity to Mrs Newman and her grief, but moved beyond any subterfuge: 'Oh, my dear, he told me to come to you. They were the last words I heard him speak, but I could not face you until I had seen him safe.'

'And is he safe?'

'Oh, yes. Quite safe and very courageous.'

'And Edward?' said Mrs Newman, raising her swollen face for an instant from Marion's shoulder. 'They say he is safe, but is it true? Have you seen him?'

'Yes,' said Charlotte and felt herself colour. 'He was quite safe, but he had a blanket about him. He had been in the water.' Beyond that she had no comprehension of what had happened.

The landing at Cologne where they were to have been so cautious, so watchful for the presence of the young soldier, occurred as in a dream. The first sight of the cathedral, so eagerly prepared for, had come too late, when it was a black established fact towering by the riverside and seeming to threaten something unexpected rather than summon up those feelings of spirituality which Charlotte and Marion had laid aside for it during the previous winter. 'Later,' said Charlotte to herself, 'when there is time.'

Now she and Ellie were included in the group of intimate sufferers. As soon as the steamer landed other people of astonishing kindness and resource took control of their lives. Without question Charlotte surrendered to their superior knowledge of what to do. Although the Hotel de Cologne was but a stone's throw from the quay, a cab was produced. Mrs Newman, Marion (become indefatigable in the care of her new friend), and Charlotte were helped into it, almost tenderly, by unknown hands. The boys were to escort Ellie on foot. A moment later they were rattling across the cobbles.

'But where is Edward?' said Mrs Newman plaintively. 'I

.

.

don't understand. If he is all right, where is he?'

'He will come to the hotel,' said Marion with decision. 'He and Mr Morrison. Never fear, we shall all be reunited soon and until that moment I promise not to leave your side.' She added in an undertone as if strangers were listening, 'There may of course be some question of the police.'

'But why?' said Charlotte.

'But you saw,' said Marion incredulously. 'There was a thief. He was giving chase to a thief.'

'And the thief was drowned?' asked Charlotte, who had indeed seen, but with no understanding.

At the mention of drowning, Mrs Newman began again to weep and Marion, compassionate and composed, delivered over her fallen head a little frown of reproach. So that when an instant later Charlotte remembered that Ellie, whom they had intended to guard with such especial strictness, had been left traipsing the streets with no protection from her suitor other than two boys scarcely older than herself, she thought better of bursting out with this new alarm. In any case the cab had already arrived at the hotel.

And does it matter, thought Charlotte with a dispassionate love of living, that the sight of the drowned man had shed temporarily over her, can it possibly matter that we allow two young people to imagine that they love one another when in two days' time they will in any event be parted?

She had found time to fear that Charles and Mr Newman would be waiting on the steps of the hotel or at least in the foyer, so that their reunion, which could not help but be emotional, would also be public. She had no taste to stand by and watch that. On arrival there was no sign of them. Instead the same kindly people who had helped them off the steamer had contrived to be already at the hotel to help them out of the cab.

'Thank you, thank you. You have been so kind,' she

seemed to say again and again as hand after hand reached to steady her elbow with a quick deferential touch of temporary love. It made her want to cry. In an hour they would all be gone. None of them she would ever know. No one would be left but the Newmans, whom she feared.

Mrs Newman, with eyes filling with tears, murmured to Marion that she had no idea what to say if the passports were requested on their arrival in the foyer, for Edward always took charge of them, and she had not even the boys to explain. 'They all speak French in these hotels,' said Marion calmingly. 'Besides, Ellie and the boys will join us directly.'

In the event there was no need for worry. Word of their situation had spread before them. There were no confusions about rooms, no awkward demands for passports. By the time they had reached the foot of the staircase leading up to their rooms, Ellie and the young Newmans appeared through the hotel door and hurried to join them. Charlotte watched Ellie closely. Was she flushed at all? Her little face wore its most enclosed look. No concern on earth it seemed could penetrate her.

Nevertheless when they were alone in their new salon she seized both Charlotte's hands in hers and drew her over to sit closely with her on a small blue silk sofa by the window. There she burst out, 'Oh, Charlotte, was that not a terrible thing? That someone should drown so close to us. Maybe we knew him, for they say he was a steward on the steamer. Maybe he helped us and we never noticed and now he's dead.'

Her face seemed masked with grief, which was fitting. For it is terrible, Charlotte thought, that someone has so suddenly stopped. Poor Ellie, she thought. I should know what to say to her, for clearly she wanted from Charlotte some reciprocal statement of grief that would sum the matter up and release her from it.

.

.

And Charlotte indeed could feel appalled that the news of this unknown man's death might even now be working its way through the invisible rattling streets below them, to the destination where it would strike true pain, despair perhaps. The delay appalled her which allowed some poor woman to move unawares about a room, preparing a meal; children to play in the sun from a window. That would be the moment of death when the words struck. What earthly good was there in thinking?

But Ellie would not let the matter drop. 'Poor Charlotte. Did you have to see him? I could not have looked. I'm sure I could not have done.'

'It was all so far away. I was so anxious for your papa—' and because with the young one must be strictly truthful, 'and for Mr Newman.'

'He was very brave. They say he jumped in to save the man. I was not sure I liked Mr Newman. He is rather moody and does not put himself about to be pleasant. Even though he was so worried about his parents, Eddie Newman put himself about to talk to me, all the way here. Tom is very shy, and I do not think I shall like him so well, but Eddie was very pleasant and so well informed about the cathedral.'

She rose and moved restlessly to the window stretching in front of it like a cat, so that Charlotte felt obliged to ask her to stand a little back into the room. So as to avert a response, she went on quickly, 'You found the younger Newmans pleasant companions, then?'

'They were pleasant enough,' said Ellie with only the slightest of shrugs. 'It might be interesting to go about in their company while we are here. Mr Newman used to live here, and of course, they speak German. Mrs Newman was so stricken. I cried when I saw her so—that they should still love one another so much.'

.

.

'Indeed,' said Charlotte. She felt reassured that the soldier had not put in his appearance.

'Of course,' continued Ellie, 'it is not surprising that she loves him. He must be so very brave. And strong. Eddie Newman says that he looked around and saw a thief.'

'Yes,' said Charlotte. 'They said there was a thief. Eddie Newman said he was one of the stewards on the steamer. He was taking Mr Newman's portmanteau right on the open deck, when everyone was looking at the raft. He threw it over the side to some accomplice in a little boat, but Mr Newman saw him and shouted out and he must have missed because the portmanteau fell in the river and was swept away, and then he saw Mr Newman and went over the side himself to get to his friend in the boat, and Mr Newman stripped off his coat and went after him down a rope. But only to save him,' said Ellie widening her eyes. 'He did not mean him to drown.'

'I should hope not.'

'Oh, no. He meant him no *harm*,' said Ellie. 'Only his friend in the boat had rowed away and he was caught in the paddles.' The frightened eager break in her voice had the power to drag Charlotte into the dark unthinkable regions below the steamer. The din. The confusion. One would whirl and batter and choke, but continue to believe in escape, in life. Then the overpowering strength of that mechanical wheel. The defeat.

But Ellie had recovered herself and went on with her tale. 'Mr Newman managed to get hold of him on the other side and swim with him round the back of the steamer and drag him onto the raft. He must be a very good swimmer.' She broke off and said, enviously now, 'But you saw it all.'

'Oh, I wish I hadn't,' said Charlotte. 'Besides, I didn't know what I was seeing. I thought Mr Newman had drowned. I thought your father was in terrible danger.'

'Was Papa brave too?' She sounded surprised.

'Yes, Ellie, surely. To go down that ladder without hesitation, to save if he could that poor man's soul.'

'Would Mr Newman have thought him brave?'

'I know nothing of Mr Newman.'

For moments the room was very silent before Ellie asked, 'Had he drowned, would Mama have been so concerned as Mrs Newman was?'

'Oh, Ellie how can you say such a thing!' And lest her meaning were not immediately clear, 'Of course she would.'

'I wonder how people love one another. How they go on loving one another. Does one know when one is in love, Charlotte? Could one mistake it?'

'Very possibly.'

'I don't believe that. I'll tell you what I believe, that no matter how strange it seemed to everyone else, that one would in some way know and that would give one strength to persist, in loving whatever happened.'

Cornered thus between love and death, there was only an attempt at truth to hold to. 'Yes. I imagine it does.'

But of whom did she speak so? The question of whether or not the soldier had waited for them at Cologne rose suddenly between them like a solid object. Charlotte found it too indelicate to ask. Yet was not it her duty to do so? No. It could not be. Better to ignore and attach no importance to it. She said instead with a formal concern, 'I hope the Newmans lost nothing of value.'

'Mr Newman lost some silver brushes.'

'Oh,' said Charlotte sympathetically.

'And they lost all their passports.'

An hour had passed when Mr Morrison flung open the door of their little salon. Charlotte had recognised his step

.

90

.

on the bare floorboards of the passage and risen from her chair. He went directly to her and embraced her. He was still trembling. The emotion of their parting on the deck of the steamer came back to them both and neither could speak.

Next he went to Ellie and folded her tightly against him. She seemed surprised at this show of feeling. 'Are you all right?' she asked, but it was a conventional question. She had not worried about him for a moment.

'Was he alive?' asked Charlotte.

'I don't know!' Her brother sank into a chair and held his head in his hands. 'They said he was dead. They'd had him over a barrel, but they took him down again. They said there was nothing more that they could do. I prayed. But he would not have understood. Yet something might have reached him. Perhaps there was some movement in the eye. Once I thought I saw some movement. I don't know.' He was silent for a moment. Then he said more briskly, 'The police will want a statement, Newman says. Above all I should have wanted to avoid contact with their tyrannical methods. Newman accepts it all too readily, but then he speaks the language and need not fear entrapping himself. Besides, he has lost all their passports and must be issued with new ones. There may be someone who must be seen. Some poor mother or even a wife who will want to know if he died in a state of grace.'

'Was he young?' asked Ellie, pitifully.

'Yes.'

'What did he look like?'

'He was well favoured enough. What a wretched business. Of all things that one would have chosen to avoid and yet Marion has been superb. The way in which she has ministered to that poor woman when she herself is so frail, surpasses praise.'

That night Charlotte found herself delaying the moment when she must go to bed. After Ellie had retired she sat for some time on the little blue sofa, staring out at the hypnotic movement of light in the dark active river. Presently she heard the throb of an approaching steamer and leant forward a little to watch it pass. First the high red and white lights on the foremast, the ring of bright flames emerging from the funnel, the yellow circles of the cabin windows. At last the single lantern at the stern.

When it was gone, her attention was caught by one particular light whose origin she could not guess at, only it seemed to suggest some warning; a red beam that pulsed like a slow heartbeat. Again and again she watched it appear, attempt to penetrate the dark water, break into fragments and fade.

She waited and in time he was with her in the room. He approached the little sofa and sat abruptly. Then without a word he forced his arm around her waist in a hard demanding embrace and buried his face against her shoulder. His hair and clothes seemed damp. She whispered angrily against his cold ear, 'Why are you here? You will catch cold.'

'Charlotte,' he moaned, 'Charlotte, my dear girl, what did you think had become of me?'

'Hush,' she said, 'hush,' for the door to where Ellie slept was half open. 'I thought you were dead.' She clung then to his head, digging her fingers into the cold damp hair, hearing her heart beat against the skull. 'I thought you were dead.'

She felt him laugh. 'Did you care then?' He raised his head to look at her, catching her chin in his cold shaking hand, turning her face to the lamplight to search her out. He surrounded her, bore in upon her, hard, wrapt in the cold wild river smell. 'I saw you in the cab. You looked quite unmoved.'

.

92

.

'I had no business being moved.'

'You are made of ice then, my cold, cold Charlotte.' No voice sounded like that in the normal light of day.

'You know I am not. You only torment me.'

'A little torment will do you good. A little pain. You make me suffer pain, Charlotte. Why should not you?'

She kept very still in fear of him, waiting. His spectral hand was on her breast. To be made to feel so was intolerable. 'Oh, this was not what I wanted,' cried Charlotte.

His lips pressed against the ridges of her ear. He ran his tongue along its outer curve. She heard the words directly inside her own head. 'What do you want then? Do you know what you want? Shall I name it to you?'

'I wanted no harm. No harm I tell you. You never believe that but it's true.'

'What harm is there in this?'

'But it is impossible. You must see that. To pretend in the day to be strangers.'

'I find no difficulty. In the day you are a stranger.'

'Won't you go away? Now.'

'I shall never go away.' And out of his great assurance he left her then to stand by the window with his back to her. A moment later he said, 'Did I kill him? Did I drive him to his death?'

'He was a thief,' said Charlotte. She trembled with his absence. 'Ellie said you were trying to save him.'

'Yes,' he said. 'That's what I seemed to think when it was over, that I had chased him to the side, but seeing him in difficulty, seeing his accomplice go off like that, that I had tried to save him.'

She went shyly to where he stood and leant her head against his back, feeling his voice vibrate between his shoulders. He reached his hands behind her waist, locking her to him.

He said, 'I drove him. I drove him to his death.'

.

.

'No,' she said softly. 'No. You know that's not so.'

'I am like that. I drive people. You can see how unhappy she is. I drive her. She is so slow. She wants nothing of life. Except to sit and me to sit and want nothing more. I can't do that. Do you understand? I can't.'

'I understand,' said Charlotte, merely to soothe. She rubbed her cheek a little on the damp back of his coat.

'But you, Charlotte,' he said, before her heart failed her, before to her despair she lost hold of him, 'you, you, you.'

Cologne

In the morning Charlotte felt unwell. Her head throbbed with threatened pain, an oppression, like the early manifestations of storm before the first shiftings of thunder. She asked Ellie to send the maid with a tray of tea and toast and planned to take it in bed. Ellie took her breakfast with her parents. She returned shortly with Marion, who was concerned.

'My poor Charlotte, I do hope you are not going to be ill—seriously ill.'

If there needed any proof of her distemper surely it was that this remark, so kindly uttered, seemed to Charlotte simply to imply that she was not ill at all, indeed was an outsider to that circle of people who knew what illness was. She said, 'I simply felt like breakfasting alone. I shall feel better presently.'

'Well, there is not all the time in the world,' said Marion. 'We are to go on an excursion with the Newmans.'

No, she thought. No. That I cannot do.

Observing her sister-in-law's set expression, Marion turned to her daughter. 'Mr Newman is a more sensitive man than I should have supposed.'

'Oh,' said Ellie. It appeared that Ellie had quite lost interest in Mr Newman, but as Marion did not address these remarks primarily to her, she continued. 'Out of consideration for his wife's nervous state, he has proposed an excursion outside the city to the Abbey of Altenburg.' She felt for the ribbon in her *Murray* and, opening it, glanced swiftly at the page as if in need of reassurance that such a place existed. 'As tomorrow is to be their last day here I thought it only civil to suggest that we form a party with them.'

'Might they not want to be alone?' said Charlotte from the bed.

'Alone! They have scarcely come all this way to be alone. Of course in some ways I am sorry to sacrifice an entire day in the city. But then Charles is so against our visiting the cathedral and so many of the relics in the minor churches seem of a somewhat morbid nature. There will be time,' she added, 'for us to shop tomorrow.'

'I shall excuse myself,' said Charlotte. 'Really I should only be a burden.'

'That is nonsense!' She waited for Charlotte to claim that it was not so that she might state more vigorously that it was. No? Then she must change position.

'I should be so afraid that Mrs Newman might take it amiss. She is a most sensitive person as we witnessed yesterday, and when she has made such a valiant effort to subdue

.

96

.

her nervous excitement and plan a day—really for the young people . . .' Seeing Charlotte's head turned on the pillow, eyes listless, she added, 'I myself have not recovered my strength, but considering what that poor soul endured yesterday and her courage in putting aside her own feelings today, I should be ashamed not to accompany her.'

'Then she will have your company. Really I am not needed.'

'Charlotte, did I not know you better I should think that an appeal for sympathy. If you will, I shall formally tell you that you are wanted.'

But nothing she could devise had power. Charlotte, now shutting her eyes, feigned a weakness she did not entirely feel, was for the first time proof against all pressures. Nothing could make her pass a day under the eyes of those people. The thought that she might betray herself by word or look, no matter how guarded, how subdued her behaviour, made it impossible. For might not he address some commonplace remark and she colour? Might not her eyes be drawn to his face without her intention and so reveal that she preyed upon him in her thoughts? Say he drew to one side and she followed. Say he pointed out some aspect of the view and she by responding before the others revealed that she had been watching him. It was quite simply impossible. She lay back on the pillow waiting for the time to wear itself away, so that they should have to go.

Marion said sharply, 'I shall have to call a doctor.'

'No. I beg of you.' It was final. An awkward silence spread about the room into which Marion resourcefully read from her *Murray.*

' "An exceedingly interesting excursion may be made to the Cistercian Abbey of Altenburg . . . fourteen miles distant. Two and a half hours' drive . . . a pathway turns off from the road a little short of Strasserhof through a glen. The distance is a very long mile. . . ." '

·

·

How it would occupy them. It would fill the day. If they would only go.

At last Marion said, 'I cannot wait. I shall have to go and make ready, but I shall be unable to enjoy myself for worrying about you.'

'Really you need not.' She added cautiously, 'How do you intend to go?'

'By cab at eleven.' There was nothing to be lost now by sounding cold and vexed. 'Now of course the young people must go unchaperoned or one of us must travel with them. Oh, well, if you will not, you will not. Come, Ellie.'

They were gone. For a time doors opened and shut. There were voices and footsteps in the passage. Then she was alone lying in silence in a room that was no part of her. The warm heavy summer air pushed in at the open window shifting the thin curtains before it. The very walls seemed to spread apart with the emptiness of the room. So light and empty was she. The pressure in her head relented. Was it possible to lie out all day in bed, watching the curtains move, the light alter on the wall? She thought not. In time there would be a maid to whom it would be impossible to explain.

She dared not stir until eleven was safely past for fear that there might be some delay and Ellie at the last be sent to check on her. From outside sounds of the street came through the window, the rumble of wheels, the clip of hooves, the meaningless excited cries of the foreign tongue, and the intimate wash of small sounds that are undecipherable in a strange place, and so seem to create a voice for it.

It would be hot in the streets. A triangle of hard blue sky came and went as the curtain blew. Idly as she lay a thin film of sweat formed between her skin and her nightdress. There was borne in upon her the luxury of being alone. And with it as the hour of eleven came and went the desire

.

98

.

to be more entirely alone. To be out among the intensifying sounds of the city. To walk in streets that formed no pattern for her, taking a turning here or there at random, as recklessly as if at any moment she should walk off the edge of the world. To see no face that could make demand of her. The beautiful blankness of faces of whom one asks nothing not even recognition. This was what she wanted.

In the glen, a little short of Strasserhof, it was cool. The earth smelt damp and sweet. The rushing stream sounded. Through the trees she heard the crushing of twigs and undergrowth, rapid, impatient footsteps, fleeing ahead? pursuing?

No, she cried to herself. No. She must not lie here a moment longer.

She washed and dressed more slowly than she was accustomed to, for all hurry is simply to accommodate someone else. No one waited. It would be hours before they might do justice to an entire abbey and return. Am I happy? she asked herself as she twisted up her hair. For what other purpose could there be to these preparations, other than to make herself happy? Rather happiness seemed too substantial a thing for her to entertain. Without the weight of those other personalities pressed against her she felt limitless, unreal.

She would go out into the street, look upwards and see the black flank of the cathedral, as she had last night from the cab, and then working this way and that through the streets, make her way towards it.

She was standing in the passage in her grey dress turning the key in its lock, tugging on her gloves with the quick furtive gestures of one who is leaving home, with nothing left to dread but some recalling voice. She would go to the cathedral and sit down. It would be cool there. Pray perhaps, because there could be no harm in it provided one was quite clear to whom one prayed. She might spend

.

.

hours there, walking a little way, sitting looking at everything twice, at last allow herself the time to feel with that exquisite sensibility which that place of all others would demand.

She handed in her key in the foyer and smiled at the porter a little direct smile that was entirely her own. She said slowly, 'How do I go to the Domkirche?' Nothing could have delighted him more. He came out onto the steps of the hotel, repeating instructions in German but also pointing dramatically to the left. So that she came to understand: a little way up the road and then off to the left. No. Not the first turning on the left. Directly on. On . . . Then the second turning to the left. That was the one to take. Did she understand? It was of such importance to him that she should.

Charlotte thanked him. Holding herself erect, walking more slowly than usual, she went down the hotel steps into the cobbled street.

Almost immediately she came to the first turning: a narrow alley, but down it she glimpsed a black broken tower, topped with jagged blocks of unfinished stone. Tufts of green grass grew between them—and the crane! How astonishing to see it first of all. To glance at random down a side alley and there light upon that segment of the whole structure on which interest must focus: the ancient crane standing on the truncated tower, the very point at which growth had ceased. The instrument which knew the day, the moment, when the last hand had stilled its movement, because the mind to which it was strung had said, 'Stop. No more,' or merely gone blank, lost faith, ceased to build.

Oh, if only Marion with her heightened sensibility were here to share this moment with her. For she felt just that mixture of awe and interest that she would have hoped to feel. And how vexing that because of her deceit she could never reveal to Marion that she had succeeded in doing so. She would write in her journal again every detail. Every shade of feeling.

Instinctively she looked back to the hotel and there stood the kindly porter shaking his head, gesturing that the way was barred. She should go on, on, directly on and then to the left. She smiled and waved. The venture had started so propitiously. This day would cure her of those evil fantasies, of that emptiness of spirit that had lately plagued her. She could hear at a distance the merry clicking of the masons' hammers. To these she timed her steps, quick, quick, quick. But why? There was no hurry. First there was this street. Its cobbles pressed the thin soles of her shoes. She said to herself, Don't hurry. There's no need. You will be there. Now you are here.

And the street seemed suddenly illuminated. She could see it all. The tall houses which had seemed quite uniform, each had its own insignia. Here there was a weaver's high window. There a crane projected from a gable like a water-spout. Sounds became particular. Quick soft tap-tap, tap-tap, were the heels of a maid servant, hurrying towards her with a covered basket on her arm and a pin like a dagger stuck through her crown of plaits.

They passed one another, their filaments crossed and snapped, severing each from the next moments of their lives, then healing on the instant with no damage done.

Slow harsh clank, clank, was the curved steel scabbard of a Prussian officer striking the cobbles as he strode ahead of her quite unaware how she cut him off from his past. Now he crossed to the other side of the street and stood outside the door to a wine house. She passed him but a few feet away. He never turned. He never noticed. She was a void, a space moving across the dense substance of the city. It yielded to her and then re-formed exactly as it had been leaving no trace of her passage.

·

·

She looked behind her and there it was quite unaltered, except that the maid servant had almost gained the end of the street and the officer had removed his helmet and was in the act of stooping to enter at the door.

Now there was another man ahead of her, wearing a tall black hat, swinging a walking stick, walking with an odd restrained gait as if he would have hurried but must not. She had followed behind him for a full minute, fitting her step in with his, when he stopped. She stopped. He tucked his stick under his arm and took out his watch. It sparked in the sun as he turned it, and turning a little as he consulted it, revealed himself.

It was impossible. He had gone to Altenburg. He had gone for the day. She had stayed behind precisely to be safe from the sight of him: Edward Newman, walking ahead of her in the street.

She was disintegrating. The edges of her void crumbled. The two sides of the street pressed in upon her. Nevertheless when he moved, she moved. Too quick and she would come up to him; too slow and he might turn a corner and be lost. Just so then, matching her pace to his, keeping in close to the house fronts lest he turn and see her, while her mind beat out explanations to the sound of her footsteps.

He had sent them ahead and would follow.

His wife had sent him back on some errand.

Perhaps like her he had declined the expedition altogether. Had his motive been the same? Had he hoped to avoid her intrusion upon him? He knew then? He had noticed?

Ahead of him she could make out the corner of the street to which the porter had directed her. And that of course was where he would turn. He too was going to the cathedral. Should she not turn back then? Just at his pace she continued to follow. She would not be denied. At the door she would wait until the vast building swallowed him up and then follow in a little while without fear of meeting him.

At the corner he continued straight ahead. But he knew the town. Perhaps there was some other way. Steadily, intently, she followed him.

To do so. To know that she did so, brought a curious relief of mind. For days with downcast eyes, stationary at tables, on benches, on donkeys, she had pursued. Now she did so in fact, feeling the prod of the cobbles step by step.

A moment later he crossed and turned down a long narrow street to the right, leading away from the cathedral. Without hesitation she followed him. He walked with the same forcedly leisured pace between the house fronts.

But he has a purpose, thought Charlotte, who, in her way, knew him. Such a man would never walk without some purpose. She would know what it was. Now as she stared at the high black hat, the black cloth coat, the purpose was there, laid out in his mind like the pattern of strange streets. She was treading the streets, sharing the purpose, partaking of his mind: Charlotte, the parasite, lodged in his brain, sucking at life, and he quite unawares.

The street was hot and airless. She had come a long way already. Sensations of fatigue brought her a little to herself. She thought, I am behaving quite strangely. If he should turn and see me, there would be no possible explanation.

He turned again to the left, down a narrow alleyway, ending in open iron gates and leaves: a park? a garden? Impossible to guess at its size.

She was more cautious now. She waited at the entrance to the alley watching him. He stopped by the gates, consulted his watch again, replaced it. Then stood, drawing his stick through his left hand, a hesitant gesture. He looked about him from side to side, into the park. For a moment he paused, rapidly tapping the calf of his leg with the stick, making some decision. Then he moved briskly forward towards the trees.

She would lose him. She moved down the alley, a shadow along the wall. Through the gates the trees formed a canopy over one of those arid, charming little squares that appear suddenly in continental cities, as urban as anything constructed out of bricks and stucco, but offering spindly metal chairs and a lace of shade. Except for Edward Newman and a woman at a table, half obscured by her parasol, it was quite empty.

Beside her three or four shallow steps led up on to a raised terrace with a balustrade and stone benches set against the rear walls of the surrounding buildings. Here she would take up her vantage point. The place was quite enclosed. He could only leave again by the gate. She could see him standing quite still with his back to her, near the tables. The rumble of wheels, the clip of hooves continued at a great distance. Nearby the only sound, the only suggestion of movement, was the flutter of doves and their low discontented cries. When Edward Newman moved several of them blundered up noisily through the trees.

He did not approach the solitary woman directly. He circled her at a distance, as if he would be sure of her face. The realisation of his motives fell on Charlotte like a blow and with it the one desire to escape from this place and see no more. Why then did she shrink back on the cold bench and continue to watch?

The woman rose quickly, lowering her parasol, and, laying it across the table, hurried towards him with her gloved hands held out. So that they caught one another by the forearm, her pale gloves on his dark jacket. His hands gripped at the elbows on her light striped dress. She raised her face as trusting as a child. He lowered his. They kissed first on one cheek then on the other. Then before she released him Charlotte could see that she had begun to talk eagerly, earnestly, pulling him back to where she had been sitting with her hand still on his jacket.

He broke away to drag another chair across the dusty ground, scattering a little flock of sparrows that had gathered watching. Seated opposite her, he rested his elbows on his knees and lightly held her hands, listening to her. Questioning. Listening. Undoubtedly she was in distress for once she freed her hands and wiped her eyes with a little handkerchief.

That they were lovers she never doubted. And of course, for he had lived in Cologne, and she had seen on the first afternoon that she watched him, that he was weary of his wife and preferred to wander off with his own thoughts: his thoughts of this square, this woman, who had turned so eagerly at the sound of her name.

Oh, this does not concern me, she thought, but still she sat where she was, too wretched with agitation to move. She could not hear their voices, nor clearly see the woman's features, but there was no mistaking the urgency with which they spoke, the directness with which they looked at one another, the protectiveness of the gesture with which he took a small packet from his breast pocket and laying it between her hands pressed his own about them. She was in tears again and struggled to hide the packet away in a little velvet bag she carried, and at the same time to extract the handkerchief and again wipe her eyes.

Now he rose and bent to kiss her. She caught at his hands as if she would detain him. All the time she spoke, beseeching? thanking? It was only possible to see the strained curve of her narrow neck as she looked up at him. No, he must leave. And so he must leave as he came and pass Charlotte by. He would be watchful as he left. There was nowhere she could hide. He could not fail to recognise her.

·

·

There was nothing to do but to rise now, while his attention was perhaps distracted and walk rapidly out of the square and back towards the way that she had come.

She regained possession of herself. She was aware of the clinging of her gloves to her hot hands, the cold trickle of sweat as she walked, the salt on her lip, no longer a void but herself as she had been, solid with a congestion of feeling that she scarcely recognised.

For Edward Newman was proved in the wrong, perjured, taken in sin, a hypocrite philanderer.

She then was exonerated.

But from what? That had been a fantasy, a dream.

Yet guilt there was. She had felt it. Though for Ellie's sake she had knelt by a succession of beds, it was a week since she had attempted to pray.

It made no difference. He could never have cared for her. There had never been any question of that. Between her and the real Edward Newman, nothing had been said. Nothing done. It did not concern her at all.

She was herself again, watching people speak inaudible words, seeing their astonishing freedom with one another. The tears, the pressure of hands, the exchange, presumably of money, were all part of a life from which she was excluded.

She walked more and more quickly. There were people ahead of her, people behind. The sound of their footsteps lapped against the house fronts like water washing against a pier. Once, behind her, sharp individual steps defined themselves, grew louder. It was he. But no. A Prussian official shouldered past, hurrying to some appointment.

That Edward Newman followed her she had no doubt. One strand of the pattern of sounds echoing off the pavement were made by his feet. It could not be otherwise. He had no other means of leaving the square. He must follow her. He must recognise her. How surely she had recognised him when his head turned a mere fraction as he held up his watch.

And now she remembered his rapid impetuous movement down the path at the Drachenfels, the sudden fearful vault over the side of the steamer, so quick and light. There was no doubt that he might overtake and accost her at any moment that he chose. If he did not do so it was because he followed her to spy out what she would do, as a little while ago she had followed him.

She had regained the wider street leading to the hotel. She would not look behind her. There was nothing to be learned but the interval at which he followed. She preferred ignorance. There was nowhere she might escape him. If she returned to the hotel he would pursue her to her room. If she refused to open her door he had only to wait.

He had said, 'I shall never go away.'

But that was different . . . inner . . . dream.

Again there rang the clear blows of the masons' hammers, like an intricate chime of little bells. She was near to the cathedral again. Above the steeply tiled roofs she could see a freshly built tracery pierced with fragments of sky. Salvation lay there in among the practical business of men jarring metal onto stone.

She took the next turning to the left down an alley so narrow that the sun could not penetrate between the tall houses. At its end was a bright open space busy with movement. Beyond she could see the cathedral like a gigantic ship tied to its mooring. Quick, quick. She did not look behind her to see if Edward Newman followed. All sounds of footsteps were lost now to the sound of hammers. Quick, quick, quick.

She was out in the sunshine again. The space in front of her was filled with red-brick workmen's huts and littered with yellow blocks of stone. Masons in their dusty smocks worked rapidly in the sun. Boys with barrows hurried between them as if the work must be completed that day. Scaffolding hung like a net, blurring the great new wall. Looking up it was possible to see tiny figures wheeling barrows across the planking and ropes slowly raising blocks of completed stone up to men waiting like pieces of carving already set in place.

On the ground the achievement seemed solid, the weight and bulk of the stones apparent, but high up there how it dwindled. How infinitesimal was the change made by one more stone. The black skeleton of the ancient cathedral still dominated. The sun shone through its bare ribs and the task of those tiny figures toiling to drag their stone shroud upwards until it might decently obscure the death, seemed hopeless.

No matter. She was safe here. The more people crowded about her the safer she was. The great south door stood open. Two streams of people passed each other going in and out. She would press in among them and lose herself, seeking sanctuary. He would never find her.

The Cathedral

Through the doors of the cathedral, she found herself in a throng of people crowded into the transept. Iron gates were shut and here they gathered pressed against the grille watching the movement of red and white as a service progressed in the choir.

It was impossible to move freely. More and more people entered behind her and she was carried inevitably forward towards the grille by their pressure. She felt invisible among them, jostled, shoved by shabby intent women with their eyes fixed straight ahead, their lips jerking and pattering in mechanical prayer. The more they surrounded her, the harder she would be to find.

She edged her way to a tall grey pillar and managed to

stand firm there with her back pressed against it and turn slightly to watch the faces behind her. There was no sign among them of the face of Edward Newman. She would stay where she was for an hour perhaps and then make her way back to the hotel. If he felt any obligation to join the rest of the party at Altenburg, he could scarcely spare that amount of time to wait.

The service came to an end. A sacristan unlocked the gate and the waiting crowd was permitted to enter and push its way forward among the stream of worshippers leaving the service. Charlotte allowed herself to be carried forward into the nave. She managed to slip aside into a disordered line of wooden chairs, there to sit a little while looking about her, before attempting the task of prayer.

The air in the cathedral was cool after the hot streets. The back of her dress, damp with perspiration, clung clammily between her shoulders. She said in a whisper, 'I should not have thought that of Mr Newman. I should have thought him at least a man of honour.' She had quite separated herself from what she had seen. It would be possible to seize Marion's hand and say in a tone of delicious anticipation, 'My dear, what I saw today! I scarcely know how to tell you, or indeed if I should at all. It will so distress you.' But that surely sounded more like Marion's voice speaking to her.

'Poor Mrs Newman has confided in me. What she has endured! We suspected something of the sort all along, did we not? I could see it in her eyes. And as you know I never felt he was entirely a gentleman. Still, I should have thought him at least a man of honour.'

Marion's voice or her own? No matter whose. It was the only voice in which such things could be discussed. But why discuss them at all? They were no concern of hers. In two days they would leave Cologne and set out for home and these people and their sorrows and betrayals would drop out of existence. If she so chose, the life at Melbury could crowd and bastion her around. If only now she could feel a little more herself.

The organ began to play, rising and diminishing in the great spaces of the cathedral. Other people's voices took their ease in her head.

Marion's: 'Of course, if he forbids us to see the interior of the Domkirche, then I for one shall honour his scruples. I have never been one to set my own will up against my husband's, but, if I were, I should be tempted to say that its essence, its true spirit is something accessible to all Christians.'

For until her brother had decreed his ban, at breakfast one morning with rain in the garden and the sudden bleak light of a wish denied, she and Marion had discussed how they should feel actually sitting side by side in the midst of this great assertion of faith rising out of the ruins of a godless age. She had said that. Marion had admired the phrase when she had used it.

Marion had said that she herself was less a high-minded woman than Charlotte, but very feeling—too feeling for her own good. It was her poor health that made her so, her awareness of the suffering of others. 'I only wish I were as robust as you, Charlotte, as sensible.' She had been so kind that afternoon. She had taken Charlotte's hand and said with her charming laugh, but quite sincerely, 'I could not contemplate entering that place with anyone but you, Charlotte.' She had gone on to describe, it was perhaps the most intimate conversation they had held, the gentle transports she would expect her sensitive nature to endure, the blameless pious raptures.

And the Magi? But there they had disagreed. Charlotte in silence, Marion with eloquence. For undoubtedly all relics were fraudulent. Who could be so gullible as to believe that these were not any three skeletons, denied a

.

111

.

decent burial, tricked out in finery so as to extract yet more money from the poor.

But what if they were not? Charlotte had thought. What if I might see those sockets from which eyes had seen . . . The thought was enormous.

The very next day, at breakfast, that possibility had been denied them by Charles; and instead she was here under circumstances she could never explain. The Magi were unimportant. She must find strength to rise and leave this place. Her brother had of course been right. He had rehearsed to them at that stormy breakfast table, after a night of wakeful prayer, the statements that the cathedral must make, fallacious, mercenary, deluding the poor and vulnerable. It was from this that he would protect them. He is afraid, Charlotte had thought in the grey rain-light reflecting off the white cloth. He is afraid his own emotions will be moved.

And he had been right to fear, although from where she sat, able to see no particular portion of the building in detail, it seemed to make no statement.

She stared at the long grey blur of pier upon pier progressing to the altar. Simply it interfered with everything as if the expanse of fretted stone were after all a filter through which the normal things of days were passed, so that they entered transformed. It confused her. She should not have come. Far from giving her peace it disturbed her. She had needed to think, to pray for help, instead she found herself unable to think clearly.

Her sight was channelled down the narrow aisle through the strange grey mist of masonry. When the sun shone in the outer world it was visible in great sparkling diagonal shafts. Tremulous disks of colour cast from the windows hovered on the surfaces of the pillars. When the sun went in, all this was instantly withdrawn and she was left with a frightened sense that the aisle had narrowed.

Indistinguishable fragments of sound washed to and fro over the expanse of stone flooring, threatening all the time to rise and extinguish the ordered sounds of the organ. With sound and sight so baffled it seemed that, at any minute, some alien and pernicious thought might lodge in her and she in confusion admit it.

So that in real fear she dropped her head directly on to her hands, for if she knelt what might she not be kneeling to? and began eagerly to pray to that God who listened over Melbury. 'From fear of our enemies, good Lord deliver us.'

But the place betrayed her. The voice which next spoke in her ear, though disembodied, was not the one that she had hoped to hear.

'What are you doing here, Charlotte? You were forbidden to come.'

Charlotte answered wearily, 'No one knows that I am here.' There was no need to raise her head from her hands.

'Your brother might walk in at any minute and discover you just as I have. Are you not afraid?'

'He is at Altenburg,' she said. 'You know that.'

'So am I,' said the voice, in which there was a new bitterness. 'Are you not afraid that I shall tell?'

Charlotte too was bitter. 'I came in because I was tired. I thought I might sit for a few minutes in peace.' Without opening her eyes she saw him, her visitant, her dream, his hands in his pockets, his legs stretched out before him so that his boots caught on the rung of the chair in front and grated it across the flags, stretched indolent in the house of God, with his watch chain slumped across his stomach. He seemed altered, the jaw fuller and the eyes—oh, something had lowered behind them to deaden any light from within and render them impenetrable.

'Yes,' she said. 'I am afraid.'

'You have been spying on me, Charlotte.'

·

·

She remembered that so well. That movement of the head as he spoke, a lifting of the full heavy chin. Just like that after all this time to remember it and the baffled feeling it induced in her, watching him so closely and having no idea what he might be thinking. How hard had been his physical presence. How he had withdrawn behind it so that she never knew at all what he might think or feel, though all the time she fretted him like a wind groping for entrance. Does he care for me? Does he care for me at all? 'Why do you follow me?' she whispered. 'Why don't you let me alone. I shall be gone in two days.'

'You followed me.'

When she did not reply, he said, 'You did not really think you could hold my attention for long?'

'I scarcely can have thought at all.' Then she said, 'I am in the habit of believing people.'

'Perhaps at least I have cured you of that. Hadn't you better go?'

'Go?' she repeated, like someone wanting release from a dream, but unable to rouse herself. 'In a minute when I feel better.'

'Oh, yes. You are pretending to be ill. You must be back in bed before they return. Poor Charlotte! It was to avoid me, wasn't it? It was quite unnecessary. I was scarcely trying to seek you out.'

'So I see.'

'I doubt you do. I doubt you are capable of seeing.'

'I saw well enough. I saw you meet that woman. I saw you give her money. I saw you kiss her. I saw you talk to her.'

'Did you imagine you had some claim on me?'

'I can see that she has the greater one.'

'Yes, but the nature of it. That is what is beyond you.'

'I am not given to gross imaginings.'

He laughed aloud then, quite regardless of where he

was. 'Are you not? That I doubt. Not given to generous actions perhaps. Not given to committals of your own precious self. But gross imaginings, as you call them, should not be beyond you. Though limited, of course, by ignorance.'

Still on her knees she turned her back upon him, gathering up her possessions, preparing to leave.

'Will you tell my wife?' He had turned her by her shoulders to look directly at him. She looked hard back at him. His face was coarse, corrupted. No one could ever have mistaken him for a gentleman.

'Is there any reason why I should not?'

'I doubt you will.'

'Why?'

'Because you are what you are.'

'What am I then?'

'You? Some sort of shadow. Really one does not consider you, more than one might a well-behaved child playing in the corner of the room.'

'You seemed to consider me.'

'Well, if the child comes forward from time to time and tries to please . . .'

'And that is all?'

'Surely that is all you have ever wanted it to be. You never risked anything. Never gave anything away. Never loved.'

'That isn't true,' she said. 'That isn't true.'

'Oh, but it is. Do you think I don't know? It's nothing but a story you tell yourself over and over again. He lifted you down from a horse. You went to some mill and thought this is the last time I shall see him. My brother doesn't approve. Marion doesn't approve. You kissed some damn flower and supposed that to be love. Good God, had you been in love, been anything but a child, it would have made no difference what they thought.'

.

.

'He was like a father to me.' She wept now into her gloves, groped in her sleeve for a handkerchief lest anyone should see. 'Marion was like a mother.'

'Are they not still? He tells you what to do, what to think. You submit and no doubt they tell you how good you are. You tell yourself how good you are. Everyone says how good you are. No one cares whether you live or die.'

'It is not wrong to try to be good.'

'It is not wrong to be timid, shallow, evasive. Only let me alone, Charlotte. You tire me.'

'And she does not?'

'Who does not?'

'The woman in the park. I saw you with her.'

'What woman?'

'You know. I saw you. I saw you with her.'

'Will you tell my wife?'

'I haven't decided.' Her final hold upon him, but it was of little effect. He shrugged as he got to his feet. 'We shall see each other often enough before you go and after that . . .' He spoke with a ringing indifference that the cathedral caught at, and flattened and deadened to deeper depths. 'After that, goodbye, Charlotte.'

Slowly she straightened her back and dried her eyes. He had gone. It is true, she thought, everything he said is true. He would come and say it again whenever he chose to pain her. If she were not safe from him here, she would never be safe. Like jack-in-the-box, like the devil, he would spring out and grab and twist while she, bonneted and gloved, moved about the streets with her basket on her arm, mended and acquiesced on the sunny window seat, at table kept her features still, walked with Ellie in the garden, avoided the shrubbery, knowing it to be empty.

She must rouse herself. There was no purpose in staying here. It was not what she had been led to expect. Charles had been right. It had deluded and betrayed her. The kings with their jewel-studded skulls were a mockery. She would not trouble with them.

All that was required of her was to stand. After that without will or effort she was drawn into the constant stream of people coming and going. She allowed herself to be carried forward by their pressures, their intentions. The organ was silent. The great wash of common sound rose, jumbling all individual prayers together, until no single cry could stand out among them. As if the vast building craved volume of sound, but cared little of what it was composed.

It seemed that she was swept by water that clamoured in her ear and permitted her no resting place, nothing to which she might grip. For a hold on any portion of the certainties which normally surrounded her would surely in a minute lift her above this confusion of drowning, but there was nothing anywhere of any familiarity. The sky, even the street, when she regained it, had an unaccountable oddness. But there at least sounds lost their distortions, were distinct from one another. Chisels rang clear. A sudden rush of bells here and there about the city announced some hour at which she could not guess.

It was possible to suppose that the men and women hurrying before her over the cobbles had identities and separate purposes. She still was who she was. She could recognise the streets. She was going towards the hotel where she would be recognised and greeted by that same porter who had been kind as she set out. And later they would return, anxious about her, loving, offering her their home, so that she cried out inwardly against the great sense of alienation that filled her. 'I have done nothing wrong. There is no reason why they should not love me.'

But there was. The only thing that kept their love was their goodness and their ignorance. If they knew

.

117

.

the thoughts that passed through her mind, even when she knelt to pray, surely it would be different. Then she thought, they must know. They cannot live so close to me without knowing that something is amiss. There must be some mark which would spread so that soon no one could mistake it.

All the time she was walking rapidly, too agitated to be open to sensation. The sour smell of the streets, the heat, the hard pressure of the cobbles, only touched her at a distance. She was urged forward by one last intention to reach the hotel, to remove this dress, to send for water and wash herself. To put on her dressing gown and climb back into bed where they would find her as they had left her, and she perhaps would be as they had left her, the time between able to exert no more pressure on the present than a dream or an imagining. So she struggled as she walked to remember the state of the present before she had set out from the hotel. Charles, safe; Edward Newman, a hero; Marion, the sudden close friend of Mrs Newman; Ellie liking Eddie Newman and free of pursuit. Towards that her footsteps pressed and pressed one after another, back along her morning track. And to that—this was the thought her mind held to—they would return.

She felt a piece of her hair against her cheek and in tucking it back into her bonnet, discovered her face to be quite moist with sweat. What must I look like? she thought. She was in the last street where she had walked behind the cavalry officer with the tapping sword. The hotel was visible at the end of it, when she was suddenly arrested by a hand laid upon her arm.

For a moment she was too startled to comprehend. The real pursuit by the real Edward Newman had been driven from her mind. Now forcibly it returned.

But it was not he. The young man stood before her earnest and beseeching as he had on the landing stage at

Bonn. Sweat studded his short upper lip. The hand which gripped her arm trembled, not with weakness but with the force of his intention. 'No,' she said before she was able to understand what he was saying, 'no. Go away from me.'

The top button of his tunic was open. She saw the strong young neck beat with the words. 'Madame, you were kind before. I mean no harm. Only her name. The name of the hotel.'

'No,' she said. 'No.'

'That I may introduce myself to her father.'

'Go away,' she said. 'Go away.' She tried to free herself of the urgent trembling hand. A woman passing turned her head. So it had come to this. She, Charlotte, raising her voice in the street to a young man she did not know.

She said again, 'Please go away. Please let me go.'

His face altered then with concern. 'I have frightened you. You are unwell.'

'Keep away from me. Do you hear? Keep away from me.'

He let his hand drop heavily then and without looking at him she began to hurry again towards the end of the street. It occurred to her that he had only to watch her for the answer to his question, that she should try to mislead him, but she was exhausted now. The only thought acceptable to her mind, filling as though it were the present reality, was that moment of safe enclosure when the door of her room was closed behind her and the key turned in the lock.

An Interview with the Police

Inside her room she found herself incapable of ringing for water. She had turned the key in the lock and would open it for no one. For a moment she stood with her back against the door feeling the brass handle press against a bone in her spine, panting audibly, pulling off the intolerable gloves. Then she moved across the room and sat down on the small blue settee. It was here that he had sat beside her and touched her.

But that was not true. None of that was true. She was quite innocent.

The truth was Edward Newman, who had addressed to her surely only the one remark, 'And you, Miss Morrison, are you looking forward to visiting the cathedral when we reach Cologne?'

Just that.

That, and the woman seated on the little metal chair in the park, who had laid down her parasol and raised her arms to him.

She shut her eyes against that vision and immediately seemed to see the red light that she had watched on the previous night, drowning and dispersing in the river.

She began to cry out loud, like a child, who, long past words, still makes a final plea for comfort. But to whom? Who was there to hear? A maid perhaps to whom she would not open the door. Rather there was the need to feel and hear the regularity of those sobs. They had become her way of breathing. The regular rasp of them in her throat was a kind of comfort. She kept her eyes closed. Warm tears forced their way between her folded lids. She saw repeatedly the red light drowning in the rush of brown water. It occurred to her then that she was in some danger; that she should do as she had intended and ring for the maid and ask for water. She tried to halt the next sob and found she could not. The sound continued like a harsh pulse. She beat to it. The red light fell in bright scallops down into the water. The weeping seemed to come from another part of the room. For a long time she sat bent over, shut in her own darkness, tormented by that solitary light, waiting for the sobs to subside.

She had not wept so since childhood. Then in her room she had hoped to be heard, listened for someone on the stairs bringing comfort and forgiveness. Tears on linen have a particular smell which she now remembered. She remembered too that there would come a time of exhaustion when it was possible to be still and sleep. Just as it had been possible in the grip of a bad dream to say: I will wake,

·

121

·

in a minute I will wake; so it was possible of weeping to say: I will stop. Inevitably, in time, I will sleep.

And so in time the room went silent. She reached behind her back and began to undo the hooks of her dress. She hung the dress over a chair and, undoing her shoes, placed them with great care side by side. The world had grown fragile and would not permit of disorder. She put on her dressing gown, took out her hairpins, and laid them in a little dish. She went into the next room, lay down on the bed, and presently, as was inevitable, she slept.

When she woke it was with a sense of total loss. She did not know where she was, nor have any self other than a mind which spoke dispassionately the words: I am going to die. That this seemed meant in general terms rather than of a particular immediate event, made it the more terrifying. There seemed no purpose in recalling the present. She lay unguarded under the weight of this idea until gradually her surroundings reclaimed her. A hotel room in Cologne. She, Charlotte Morrison. Ellie sitting on the opposite bed watching her. A great peaceful desolation.

Ellie said, 'Are you all right?'

She was a little pale. From walking in the heat perhaps. She had taken off her bonnet and dangled it over the side of the bed by its pink ribbons, her hair was pinned tightly back behind her ears. Her frock, cotton, pink, sprigged with little brown flowers, was an old one from previous summers, a favourite which Charlotte had lengthened, covering the white mark of the old hem with a narrow band of brown velvet ribbon. The faded colour, its tightness—she could see where the narrow cuffs dented the full flesh of Ellie's arm—gave her a touching childishness. How pretty she is, thought Charlotte, how sweet. She said, 'Yes. I have been asleep.'

'Have you been out?'

'Why do you ask?' For suddenly she remembered enough to be cautious.

'Only I saw your dress.'

'I thought I might go out. I started to dress, but I felt too unwell. I slept for a while.'

'I thought you had been crying.'

'No,' she said. 'No. Of course not. I felt rather sick, my head ached.' Not only was it possible to lie, it was immaterial whether Ellie believed her or not.

'Is your head better now?'

'I feel very tired,' said Charlotte. It seemed an acceptable term for the sense of blankness that filled her. 'But my head is better.'

Ellie said timidly, 'We went to Altenburg, to the abbey.'

'Oh, yes,' said Charlotte, rousing herself to sit up cautiously against the pillows. 'Did you enjoy the abbey?'

'Oh, it was pleasant enough.'

'You had the Newmans for company?'

'Yes,' she said, expressing in her tone of voice a great absence.

'You like them, don't you?'

'They are pleasant enough. Mr Newman could not come.'

'Indeed?' said Charlotte, turning her head on the pillow.

'He had to go to the police about the man who drowned and Mrs Newman talks all the time to Mama in a confidential way so that I am not included.'

'And the young men?'

'Oh, they are well enough. But they are very young. Tom Newman is still at school and though Eddie Newman goes out to business, it is only his father's business and he lives at home with his mother to care for him, so you could not call him entirely a man really. Besides he is so polite that he makes me feel clumsy. Poor Charlotte, are you very tired? Your eyes look swollen. I thought you had been crying.'

'So you said.'

She twisted the pink bonnet ribbons between her fingers. 'When I came back I cried a little because the day had been so very disappointing.'

'Oh, surely not,' protested Charlotte to shield herself from this candour.

'He was not there, Charlotte. I thought surely from what you said that he would be in Cologne, waiting on the landing or in the streets somewhere. Even at Altenburg, although of course he could not have known that we should be there. I thought my heart would break when Mama said we must be out of the town for a whole day.'

'Who do you mean?'

'Oh, Charlotte, you know!'

'You are to forget that foolish incident.'

'I cannot.'

'But it was nothing.'

'I cannot forget him. I think and think about him. Can you remember his face?'

'No. I cannot,' said Charlotte all the more sharply that on the instant she did.

'But you have seen him more recently than I, and I can remember him as if I had known him a long time.'

'You saw him only for a moment,' said Charlotte.

But Ellie was not to be held at a distance. She moved now impulsively to sit on Charlotte's bed, but looked a little past her as she spoke as if she were talking aloud to herself. 'There were so many people in the streets, wearing uniforms, and each time I thought it might be him but each time I knew in my heart that it was not. I know him so well that I should know it was he even at some distance. Do you believe that possible?'

•

•

Does it matter what I believe, thought Charlotte. She said, 'I wouldn't know. I think you imagine it.'

'But if we did see him even in the distance, it would be of some significance, would it not? There could be no other reason that he would come to Cologne other than to see me again.'

'Ellie, we know nothing of him. There could be a thousand reasons.'

'But I feel I know, Charlotte. It may seem very strange, but I feel I will see him again. Perhaps I will not and then I shall feel very foolish to have said this to you, but it helps me to talk about it.' The room had darkened so that it was possible to talk so, almost impersonally out of no particular existence to no particular being. 'I could talk on and on. It's so long until tomorrow.'

'What time is it?'

'Seven o'clock.'

'I have slept so long.' Inside her head the day had begun to reassemble itself.

'The police are with the Newmans.'

'Why is that?'

'Oh, it is to do with the man who drowned.'

'But surely you said he saw the police earlier today.'

'Now they want statements from us all.'

'All?'

'Yes. I think you'd best get up if you are able.'

'But why, Ellie, surely it is no concern of ours.'

Before she could answer there was a soft tap on the door and Marion came into the room. 'How gloomy you have it here,' she said, automatically straightening the brushes on the dressing table as she passed. 'Put the lamp on, Ellie.' To Charlotte she said not at all unkindly, 'I trust you have recovered yourself.' There was an air of haste, an importance about her, that had been missing during the summer. It shielded her from the fragile atmosphere of the room

.
125
.

and caused her to look less searchingly at Charlotte than she might have done. Nor did she appear to notice that her question, if such it were, remained unanswered.

'You had best hurry. The police wish to see us in our rooms in half an hour.'

'But I have no evidence,' protested Charlotte. 'Surely I need not be included.'

Her sister-in-law did look at her now with a little frown. 'Why, you above all, Charlotte, who were actually on the deck watching while I was below with poor Dorothy Newman. You should have more to relate than any of us.' She left a second's pause, but when it was not taken up, pursued, 'I personally feel that we should insist on having Edward Newman at our interview so that there can be no exchange of German between them—there are always two of them, you know—that we do not fully understand.'

'I can't,' said Charlotte. 'I can't.'

'But you must. Charles particularly mentioned that we should all be together as a family.'

'I can't. I saw nothing. Please just leave me.'

'But what is the matter with you?' The skin between her eyes creased like tissue paper. The little mouth grew set and tight as she approached the bed and looked down at Charlotte. 'I have never seen you like this. Are you ill?'

'Perhaps.'

'Then I insist again that we send for the doctor.'

'Oh, no.'

'Then you must wash your face and straighten yourself and come. Charles was most displeased when you failed to accompany us this morning, and what was I to say to Mrs Newman? I could hardly claim that you were ill—too ill to come out—when patently that was untrue. Nor could I very well claim that you were more upset by yesterday's proceedings than she or I.'

'What did you say then?'

'I could only tell the truth, that you were not yourself and wished to spend the day alone.'

She paused for this to take effect. But what effect was taken? Her sister-in-law's face was wan and impassive. Then in a moment she was all decision and movement. 'Quickly. They cannot be much longer with the Newmans.' She snatched back the coverlet revealing Charlotte laid out straight and unmoving in the narrow bed. 'Oh, quickly, Charlotte. You look such a spectre I am ashamed of you.'

She had her by the arm. It was useless to resist. As Charlotte lowered her feet over the side of the bed, she noticed how white they were as if they had not been used for years. Apart from that she took no interest in the proceedings. Marion was saying, 'Quickly, Ellie, the eau de cologne, while I do her hair.'

She sat obediently at the dressing table watching them work upon her in the glass. The feel of other hands about her was neither intolerable nor soothing. Merely they seemed to batter softly at her for purposes of their own. There was no refusing them. She allowed Ellie to bathe her temples and Marion in a final assault to pinch her cheeks as if she were some sickly child about to be brought to table. Then they hurried her to the Morrisons' salon.

Mr Morrison sat at the table busily writing his statement. He sat as all his life he had sat at desks and tables first in this house then in that; writing sermons, letters, keeping accounts, but always the posture the same, his elbow propped by his writing, his veined freckled hand supporting his chin, the long strands of grey hair falling between his fingers, the absorption in the task. Charlotte took a chair at a little distance from him with her back to the light, watching dispassionately the degree of business he contrived to put into his writing, the seriousness, the importance. When he had finished he read it through, crossing a word here, inserting a few rapidly there. Then he replaced the pen carefully, sanded the final page and looking from one to another of them as if they were an expectant audience said, 'That is the truth as I see it.'

He too, Charlotte noticed, had an air of purpose that he had lacked all summer. Fate had given him in the drowned person of the thief what he had so sadly missed, a kind of parishioner.

His wife sent him a little smile that seemed to jerk her head in a nod of approval, but all she said was, 'I wonder what class of man would a policeman be in Prussia.' She was preparing in all its minutest subtleties her greeting of this person who would shortly knock on the door.

'Everyone in Prussia is educated,' Ellie put in, 'Eddie Newman says.'

'Many most surprising people in England receive an education these days,' said her mother, 'but there is little significance in that.'

Mr Morrison said, 'I doubt he will be just an ordinary policeman. After all a crime against a British subject is no small matter. They are sure to attach importance to it. They are sure to send some quite senior official.'

Unconsciously they had grouped themselves in a semi-circle facing the door and spoke to one another in this slightly public manner with those minute but perceptible pauses between each remark that indicates discomfiture of some sort.

'It is curious,' said Mr Morrison, 'that there should be no mention at all of the incident in the local newspaper. I had Newman look especially, but he said there was not a trace of it. He scarcely seemed surprised. The repressive censorship of the press is one of the most regrettable aspects of this regime, quite at odds with the intellectual pretensions of the court.'

'Perhaps there will be something tomorrow,' said Ellie.

·

·

'Perhaps it will say who he was and if he had a wife and children.'

'Oh, Ellie, do not dwell on it,' said her aunt from where she sat.

'Still, I should like to know. Would not you, Charlotte?'

'No,' said Charlotte. 'No. On the whole I should not. There is little to be gained by knowing. What could we do?'

'I intend to ask this man what information they have,' pursued her brother. 'Of course I should feel it my duty to visit her. Whatever her husband's trade, she might herself be a devout and innocent woman, who might obtain some comfort from knowing that he was not alone when he died. That the last sound he heard on earth was the sound of prayer, which surely is unmistakable in any tongue. That his soul was bombarded at the last with entreaties to repent.'

'But he was dead,' said Ellie. 'You said he was dead.'

'Sometimes the soul lingers when all sign of life is withdrawn. There is never any justification for doubting that one's final prayers have failed to reach their destination. Or that the heart most hardened in crime may not relent in the final moments of life. I have seen it happen,' he said eagerly to his wife.

But she was in no mood for reminiscence. The present ran too strong in her this evening. Already it felt strange to gather formally like this without the company of the Newmans. She said to Mr Morrison, 'Were we wrong to agree to see this man alone? Might it not be wiser to include Edward Newman with his knowledge of the language?'

'If the inspector speaks no English, it will be necessary.'

His tone seemed favourable. She went on, 'Even if he speaks a little, might it not be safer? One might so easily be trapped into statements one had never meant. I believe they are very cunning.'

'But, my dear, what purpose would they have in entrapping me? I saw nothing of the crime. Only its tragic consequence. Indeed I wonder they wish to see me at all except as a check on Newman's statement. They must have chosen me as a reliable source of the plain unvarnished truth and with that they can do very little beyond making a copy of what I have written here.'

Though he had not exactly agreed with her, Charlotte could see that her sister-in-law was scarcely displeased. She smiled her small contained smile, smoothed the plush cloth with her hand, and then with a tilt of her head and a more public smile, her hair. She was preparing to be a hostess again: to receive to her abode admittedly a mere policeman, but a senior policeman. When it was over there was a friend in Dorothy Newman to whom she could relate it all.

Presently the knock came. The policeman entered, a sparse, scarcely smiling man who would, it appeared to Charlotte, have disappeared altogether had he been able, the better to observe the other people in the room. His bow, the scarcely audible click of his heels, were small things pared to a minimum. He said in English that was accented but clear, 'You are Mr Morrison.'

'I am.'

Behind him was a younger man, slight, dark, with a thin clever face. With a silent bow for which he seemed to expect no response, he went to the table. Would everyone excuse his sitting, he asked them with his eyes, and when he was ignored, sat and placed on the plush cloth a battered leather writing case from which he briskly produced a stack of paper and a bundle of pens. He was ready. He sat with his hands folded on the paper looking from one to the other.

'Won't you sit down?' said Marion to the inspector. Her

smile was charming, a thing of past prettiness, that made him bow again, a shade more profoundly. He took his seat at the table, spreading his coattails. The secretary sat quietly opposite, waiting.

'You have prepared a statement?' the inspector asked Mr Morrison.

'I have.'

'Then with your permission I shall read it now and give it to my colleague here to translate.'

'I shall sign nothing,' said Mr Morrison with commendable firmness, 'written in a language I do not comprehend.'

The inspector eyed him sharply. 'Your friend, Mr Newman, wishes to attend our interview to assist with the language. Do you object?'

'I do not,' said Mr Morrison, gravely proferring his statement.

Holding it in his hand, the inspector rose, opened the door, and called into the passage, 'Will you come, Mr Newman.'

Footsteps. Voices. The closing of the door. Charlotte's clasped hands in the grey lap of her dress. She would not look up. Silence fell in the room, broken only by the small movements of obscurely anxious people. The statement was being read.

At last the inspector said, 'You express yourself very clearly. I think we shall understand one another, Mr Morrison.'

Only then did Charlotte raise her eyes to where she knew Edward Newman must still be standing by the door. A heavy man, with a moist face, an overattentive look in his eye. She thought, I am free of him. I know what he is. That is all past. I pity his wife, but it is no concern of mine.

The inspector was saying to Marion, 'I believe you saw very little of these events.'

'I noticed nothing amiss until Mrs Newman screamed and fainted. Naturally from that moment my thoughts were entirely taken up with her welfare.'

She was enjoying this, Charlotte could see, like a child who has prepared the lesson well and can count on approval.

'She told me,' the inspector said, with a near smile, 'how kind you were. Your daughter too was with you?'

'All the time.'

'That is so, Miss Morrison?'

'That is so,' said Ellie shyly.

'And you have a sister, Mr Morrison?' But he had taken her in when he entered the room. It was merely a device that he seemed to seek her out among the small number of people present. 'You are also a Miss Morrison?'

'I am.'

'And you were with the other ladies?'

'No,' said Charlotte. 'There seemed to be a number of ladies in attendance on Mrs Newman. I remained on the deck.'

'Why was that?'

'I wished to understand what was happening.'

'And naturally you were concerned about your brother?'

'Not at first. I was unaware that my brother was involved.'

'You say at first. What was the first moment at which you were aware of these events?'

She could hear the rapid scratch of the secretary's pen. Her words, but written in forms she could not understand. 'I saw Mr Newman run across the deck and jump over the side.' He would be looking at her now.

'And what seemed the explanation for this action?'

'There seemed no explanation.'

'You could not see the thief?'

'No.'

'Nor the portmanteau he is said to have cast over the side?'

'No.'

'What more did you see?'

'Nothing. Nothing—everyone pressed about me so—until I saw the man over the barrel on the raft. Then they called for a priest and my brother went to them. I watched him as long as I could see him, and then I went below.'

'And in all this did you see anything of Mr Newman?'

'I saw him stand a little apart with a blanket over his shoulders while my brother administered to the dying man.' Suddenly it was possible to raise her eyes to Edward Newman's and meet his levelly. Was there a movement in them, some anxious alertness?

'You are sure at that distance it was he?'

'Oh, yes, perfectly sure,' said Charlotte to Edward Newman.

'And of course you could not corroborate Mr Newman's statement that he kept his family's passports in the portmanteau.'

'Of course not.'

'That is all then. Thank you, ladies. Thank you, Mr Morrison.'

'You want no more of us?' said Charles. His tone was almost slighted.

'Thank you. That is all.' Again the minimal bow and the touch of the heels. The secretary had risen and maneuvred into position to leave last through the door. 'We shall send the translation for Mr Newman's approval and your signature later tonight. You may keep the original.'

'But I wish to know more,' said Charles. 'There has been no account of this in the papers. Why is that?'

The inspector shrugged. 'As I said to your friend, it is lamentable but there are so many of these petty thefts on the river that they are scarcely news. Besides, the river boats are a world of their own. The people on them do not necessarily come from Cologne.'

'But surely you know his name and where he came from. If he had a family in the city I should feel it my duty to visit them.'

'We have been unable to trace any identity. The name he had given the shipping company was apparently assumed. Regrettably this is often the case.'

'So you will drop the matter? You consider it too trivial to proceed with?'

'On the contrary, the loss of an English passport is a very serious matter. It will be investigated most thoroughly, but your concern in the matter, Mr Morrison, may end here. You acted with courage and did all that you could. I hope that the unfortunate incident need not cloud the final days of your visit.'

He and the secretary were rapidly through the door before they could devise other words to detain them. They left behind them a sense of disappointment. It seemed that the English party felt cheated of their full share of attention, excluded perhaps from some drama.

This Marion now tried in some part to rectify. 'That other was a policeman too—that little man. There are always two of them—for confessions.'

'But, my dear, they can scarcely have expected to wring confessions from us,' said her husband mildly. 'Still, I find the secrecy of their methods thoroughly distasteful. Presumably their true motive in keeping this out of the papers was to disguise from foreign visitors the true nature of the risk they run. I trust'—he looked sternly about at the women dependent upon him—'that this brings home to you the precious nature of our English freedoms.'

'I thought,' said his wife, presumably by way of some sort of answer, 'that we all acquitted ourselves very well—even you, Charlotte, who had been so reluctant to come.'

•

134

•

It was curious that Edward Newman did not excuse himself, but remained by the door, where he had stood throughout the interview, propping his arms on the back of a chair with his head slightly bowed so that he looked neither comfortable nor in any way prepared to move. It seemed there was something more to be said on the subject, though surely now it had been exhausted.

Yet he did not leave though a sudden silence had fallen upon them. Charlotte felt across the room his alien hardness, his unapproachability. If he would not go, she would have him look at her.

She said, 'What is the significance of the passports being lost?'

'Oh, that is an irrelevance,' said her brother.

But she had succeeded. She held Edward Newman's eye. Indeed he watched her closely as he answered her—as if she puzzled him.

'Cannot you guess, Miss Morrison?'

'I should not ask then.'

'An English passport commands a high price.'

'But why?'

'Your brother has just reminded you of our superior English liberties. There are many people in this country who have offended the authorities and who face imprisonment if they cannot escape to a more liberal country. An English passport can be their one means of escape. This summer when such numbers are travelling through Hamburg to the Great Exhibition, the authorities at the port are so pressed they have a chance of escaping detection. It is that that is exercising him, the fear that this man was no ordinary thief, but was engaged in a traffic which might help political offenders to escape his net.'

'Then perhaps you will agree, sir,' said Charles Morrison, 'that some good may come out of this wretched business, if tyranny is in any way thwarted.'

'I believe that my passport like the rest of my possessions lies at the bottom of the Rhine. Do not you, Miss Morrison?'

Why should he single her out? Why press her so?

'It is of little moment,' she said, 'if the authorities have issued you with new ones.'

'They had no choice but to do that.'

'Quite so,' she said rising, for really if he would not go, she must. He held the door for her and watched her again with that same look of sharpened speculation.

So that she thought, with a tremor of alarm, Our roles are reversed. Now it is he that pursues me.

A Quarrel

It was true. She was done with imagining. He pursued her with some motive she could not guess at. I drive people, he had said. But no. He had not said that at all. Nevertheless when, on the following morning, there was finally mounted the expedition to buy eau de cologne, it seemed more than a coincidence that he so obtruded upon her.

It was the simplest of purchases for, once they had decided that they should go to Farina's in the Julichs Platz rather than to Zalnoli's, there were few decisions left to make. Mrs Newman, who had sisters in Derbyshire absolutely depending upon her, felt quite justified in purchasing a crate of six bottles which was after all known to be the most economical and practical way to convey it home.

The idea of two crates was toyed with but discarded as excessive. Besides, they would be sure to return. Her husband would never rest until they returned. Sometimes, she added wistfully to Marion, she thought he loved his summers in Germany more than his own home.

Marion, on the other hand, might never visit Cologne again. It was only concern over her health that had induced Charles to leave his parish for so many weeks. She could not ask him to make such a sacrifice of conscience again whatever her condition. So two crates or one?

That morning at breakfast she had tried to persuade Charlotte that two would be practicable if she would take a share, but Charlotte had again proved awkward. She was prepared to risk the near certainty of breakage to return home with only one small bottle for herself and a slightly larger one for an old friend. And all because of this capriciousness Marion must have less than she wanted or more than she wanted. In the end more than she wanted seemed, she said, the most sensible, taking into account her incurable generosity and the number of people who would expect something on her return.

After such forethought the time actually spent in the shop was comparatively short. The three crates were produced and the two bottles of separate size for Charlotte.

Simple as it all was, twice Edward Newman intervened on her behalf in German. The label on her bottle was slightly damaged it appeared. Another was produced with apologies. Was that exactly the size she wanted? It appeared there were a great many different sizes. Several times, it seemed as she made her final purchase at a counter, his blunt hands and his heavy gold rings moved across her vision.

Had she simply agreed to take her share of Marion's extra crate she could have avoided all this. It was her awkwardness that laid her open to his attentions. For she was a little withdrawn from true centre as he was. Perhaps he recognised in her that slight discomfiture he must know in himself. She roused herself to listen to her sister-in-law and Mrs Newman and to appear to be at one with them as they exclaimed over the medal of the Great Exhibition in London, stamped upon the bottles.

It was proposed that the crates should be sent back to the hotel by cab. Tom Newman, always obliging, was to go with them and the others were to stroll through the streets at Mr Newman's direction, returning to the hotel in time to prepare for the table d'hôte at noon.

Charlotte walked ahead with Ellie. Her niece was very silent. Eddie Newman had done his best all morning to engage her in conversation, but now he seemed to have lost heart and fallen back with his father. The soldier had not reappeared. Of that Charlotte was certain, for among her other preoccupations she had looked constantly for him. She made no attempt at talk. What was there to say other than to confess how finally she had dismissed that poor young man? And this she found she had not the courage to do.

There were quickening footsteps behind them, and Ellie, ever watchful, turned and stood aside a little. Eddie Newman and his father were approaching them.

Charlotte hoped that by standing still she could avoid them and attach herself to the ladies behind. But although the young man addressed some remark to Ellie and fell into step beside her, his father hesitated as if he felt it impolite to proceed without her company.

After a pause he said, 'Will you wait for your sister-in-law?'

'Yes,' said Charlotte briefly, and looked not at him but back down the linden avenue to where Marion and Mrs Newman had fallen behind, arms intertwined, dark travelling skirts as one, bonnets inclined at a slight angle towards one another, deep in conversation. She added, 'I am a little fatigued.'

'Indeed.' The silence between them seemed drawn to intolerable lengths. Still she would do nothing to break it.

He said, 'You chose to walk in the city yesterday rather than in the country with the rest of your party. Perhaps that has tired you?'

The whole seemed phrased as a question, yet she doubted that it was. She thought, he knows. He saw me. She looked him directly in the eye then as long years of telling the truth had taught her to do without embarrassment and said, 'I spent the day in my room.'

It was necessary to continue looking at him, so that her eyes might not appear to waver, so that she might attempt to read in his face the effect of her remark. For a moment he watched her with interest, she thought with a kind of admiration. Then his irregular smile slowly raised the corner of his mouth. She could hear his wife's footsteps and Marion's approaching, sharply punctuating the murmur of their talk.

He said, still smiling, 'If you had been tempted out to see the cathedral, I should respect your secret.'

'But I was not.'

'Quite so,' he said, as the others joined them.

It must be admitted that they were less sedulous tourists than they had been at the start of the summer. The main business of the day being accomplished, it was agreed that the ladies should take a little nap after their meal. Edward Newman and his sons were bound for the cathedral. Charles had indicated that he wished to read a book.

The afternoon was really spent by the time Charlotte and Ellie repaired to the elder Morrisons' salon, but there they found that Marion had a plan for their entertainment.

'I have,' she announced, 'arranged with Dorothy Newman that we all go together by cab this evening to Deutz across the river and sit for a while in the gardens there.'

There was the slightest pause while she gauged the reactions of the people to whom she proposed this treat which was by now unavoidable. Then she proceeded a little defensively, 'Dorothy says it is a delightful entertainment, the pleasantest to be had in Germany and very reasonable.'

Only her husband said, over the edges of his book, that he would find it the more pleasant if they were not detained too late; but each for their several reasons failed in their response. Perhaps in irritation at their indifference Marion said in a voice grown aimed and penetrating, 'I doubt Charlotte will be pleased at my suggestion.'

It is scarcely that, thought Charlotte, but held her peace. She had returned automatically to the little gilded chair she had occupied during the interview with the police and sat quite still as she had then with folded hands.

'Why should she not?' said Charles vaguely.

'Because it is all too apparent that she does not care for the Newmans' company.'

He lowered his book unhappily and turned a wary glance from his wife to his sister. Like a child who senses from his parents' tone that against all the laws of nature they are angry with one another, he assumed a furtive look as inwardly he sought for shelter.

'Do you dislike the Newmans?' he asked Charlotte. 'I had the impression that you were rather friendly with her.'

Now Marion kept silent and she must answer. 'I have scarcely had time to decide whether my feelings are friendly or not. On the whole I suppose they are.'

'Is your friendship of such moment,' said Marion, 'that you must spend days deciding where best to bestow it? If so you will be too late, as we part tomorrow.'

'I suppose that is what I mean. It has been too brief an acquaintance to feel one way or another.'

•

•

'I have not found it so, but then perhaps you would say I give my sympathies too readily.'

'No,' said Charlotte. 'I would not say that.'

'Meaning?'

'Meaning that I should not accuse you of being too ready with your sympathies.' But however she answered, the question had been pitched in a tone that signalled clearly that a quarrel was intended and, because such things have their own formality, each immediately took up a position.

Ellie sighed heavily and left the room, shutting the door with an emphasis that formed the only comment she was allowed. Charles moved to stand by the window, back to the room, wretchedly hunching his shoulders. Marion settled back in her chair and lifted her canvas work, concentrating upon it as she said, 'I fear Charlotte will find the company we keep at Melbury tiresome.'

Silence. As no one had been addressed directly, no one answered.

'I fear,' she went on, 'that Mr Ransome must have been somewhat reclusive in his habits and that you have got out of the way of talking to people.'

'I lack your gift,' said Charlotte, 'for talking to people.'

'It is scarcely a gift. Charles knows,' she directed to his back, 'if you do not, that by nature I am very reserved, but I have always felt it my duty to be pleasant to people with whom I am thrown into contact.'

'You cannot accuse me, surely,' said Charlotte, 'of being unpleasant to Mrs Newman.'

'Not unpleasant,' she conceded. 'Of course not actively unpleasant, but'–and here she must search–'more indifferent; as if her affairs were no concern of yours.'

'Well?' said Charlotte so that her sister-in-law was goaded forward.

'To him you are positively abrupt. Surely in the last

.

.

fifteen years you have had some occasion to make conversation with gentlemen?'

'Little enough,' said Charlotte. And here there opened up so many paths down which the next remark might precipitate that for a moment they were silent.

Finally Marion said, 'Well, it will not be so at Melbury, will it, Charles?'

He chose, as he must turn, to appear to have lost the thread of the discussion and looked from one to another with a kind of cautious bewilderment.

Charlotte said, 'Perhaps you would prefer I stayed behind tonight. There will be ample company for Ellie.'

'Ah. I was wondering when you would propose that. It was sure to come. That is the very point I would make and must unavoidably.' She addressed her husband. 'If Charlotte is to make her home with us, it is necessary that she be agreeable to everyone whom we meet, whether or not they are of interest to her.'

It was the first condition. She turned involuntarily to her brother.

'I am sure she will be,' he said.

There was such pleading in his voice, such a longing for peace, that Charlotte felt contrite.

'Of course I shall come this evening.'

'I am glad,' said Marion. 'I should have been hard put to it to claim that you were ill a second time.'

Something in the voice dismayed Charlotte to the point of rising and standing directly before her brother, so that she might intercept any answer that he might give. She said, 'I do often feel ill, find company exhausting for reasons I cannot explain, wish very much to be by myself. Perhaps this unfits me to live with others.'

It seemed a plea for pastoral advice and as such he could not resist it. 'You will have your times of private prayer. And you would do well to devote some of that time to praying to accommodate yourself to the needs of others. Solitude spent without the discipline of prayer only breeds a morbid self-pitying frame of mind.'

'Which tendency we have noticed in you, Charlotte,' put in her sister-in-law. 'I myself have always found true happiness in the service of others. In giving and not receiving.'

But Charlotte ignored her, singling out her brother. 'How much time will you permit me for private prayer?'

'That is surely a matter for your own conscience.'

'But I wish to know exactly, before I take this step.'

'What step?'

'That of deciding whether to live with you.'

'But that has been decided.'

'It has not been entirely decided.'

'But we spoke of it on Drachenfels. It has been the subject of my earnest prayer. We have agreed.'

'We?'

'Why, all of us.'

'I have not agreed,' she said.

'You are exciting yourself to no purpose. We spoke of it on Drachenfels when you were calmer and you agreed entirely that you could not live alone.'

'You wept,' said Marion.

'Then I cannot have been entirely calm.'

He said, 'There is no alternative.'

'I could live alone,' she said eagerly. 'With the money Mr Ransome left me, I could rent a little cottage and furnish it simply. With care I could manage.'

'If you wish to isolate yourself,' said Marion. 'If you wish to live solely for your own comfort, there is very little we can say to dissuade you.'

'Perhaps you would rather not dissuade. Perhaps you would rather that was what I did.'

'Nobody has ever given you cause to say that.'

'Perhaps I can guess at your feeling. Perhaps I remember the past.'

'Oh, this is most distressing,' cried her brother. 'Everything in the past was done for your own good; because you did not know your own mind and needed decisions made for you.'

'I think Charlotte does not know her own mind now,' said his wife.

'I knew it better then.'

'I for one am finding this intolerable,' said Marion. She rose deliberately, collected up her canvas work, and made a slow departure which they could only stand and watch until the lock clicked crisply behind her.

'You have distressed her,' said Charles reproachfully. 'You know how precarious her health is.'

'And mine is not?'

'No, yours is not. If you are to live with us, you will have to consider her more.'

'If?' she said. 'If? I thought it was decided. I thought there was no alternative.'

'You are tired,' he said. 'You are not yourself.'

'Who then? Look at me. Who?'

'My sister of whom I have always been very fond.'

'Until now. Until this minute.'

'There is no purpose in pursuing this. You are overwrought—overtired. It will pass. You will see. We shall all go on as we were.'

'Do you wish me to withdraw now to my bed? Or do you wish me to accompany you and make myself pleasant to Mr Newman—Mr Newman!' she repeated, as if the name were an enormity.

'I wish you to retire to your room. In time prayer will bring you to a more reasonable frame of mind. Your duty, I need not remind you, is to Ellie, and I gather from Marion that you have not been altogether zealous in its pursuit.'

'Oh, but I have,' she said. 'I have done all that either of you could wish for.'

'What do you mean?' It pleased her that she alarmed him.

'I mean that I have spoken to that young man again. That I have been just as crushing of his hopes as you would wish me to be. That I have shown no pity to Ellie. You would have been proud to see how well my lesson was learned.'

He actually covered his ears with his hands. He said, 'I cannot listen to this. It means nothing to me. If you will not leave the room, I must.'

'I shall leave.' She walked towards the door with a curious lightness of heart. It occurred to her that she was no longer entirely alive, and that she felt the better for it.

TWELVE

An Evening in a Beer Garden

Now she dressed again. Charlotte the deceased; the late; the former; present only in the glass; plaiting her hair. Her thumb and forefinger were rapid, the other fingers lifted in a quick repeated gesture so that her mother's ring glinted. Charlotte, watching the ring's reflection, said without a sound, 'How many more times shall I do this? Once? A hundred times? A thousand? What matter. Dead mother. Dead ring. Dead Charlotte. All quite, quite safe.'

No need to mention it. No alteration in the glass to the thing they were accustomed to see. Neat, smooth. No trace of death. Only an intense quiet.

Now must come the preparation to leave the room. Gloves. Shawl. Reticule. Bead upon bead. Two hours at most and then return to the room. Loosen the dress, loosen the hair. Lie down. No fear of visitants. Sleep. Blank: her new element.

Now along the corridor, down the stairs, Ellie alive beside her. In the foyer, the Newmans. Mrs Newman seated on a red plush settee as if she would never rise: he paced to and fro. He looked at her as she approached, perceiving no change. But Charlotte, in a triumph of negation, saw him and felt no tremor. At so little cost then had she escaped him.

'Good evening, Miss Morrison.'

'Good evening.'

'Good evening.'

'Good evening.'

In the cab she sat among the young people: Ellie beside her; the two boys opposite. Each applied his face to the window nearest as if each were involved in a separate search. They had nothing to say to one another. Well, they must learn for themselves. She would not help. She leaned against the leather seat, letting the cab shake her and sway her while she closed her eyes and chose instead to explore the limits of her new condition. She could feel the unnatural stillness of her hands in her lap.

She heard Eddie Newman say in a low conspiratorial voice almost as if he hoped she slept and would not hear, 'Would your father allow you to climb to the roof of the cathedral? Tonight when we return? There will be a moon. It would be a splendid sight. Surely he could not object. It is only a view.'

She said indifferently, 'I could ask. If Charlotte would come with me.'

'Why, certainly,' said Charlotte, opening her eyes, looking at them. Eddie Newman sat forward on his seat. Light from the street fell intermittently on his face revealing a rapt intent look towards the corner where Ellie in her pale shawl shone like a moth on a dark leaf.

'You would enjoy it,' said Tom Newman kindly to Charlotte. It was he who was good to his mother.

'No doubt,' said Charlotte, but really it was unfair to speak coldly when he was so young and needed to please. She straightened herself on the seat and smiled at him, and he smiled back, shy and delighted to have given pleasure to anyone.

'Will your father allow you to dance?' pursued his brother ardently to the corner of the cab.

'Oh, yes.' Her light bleak voice seemed to float in at the window. Isn't it always so, it seemed to say. We are going to a garden, by a river, lights, music, there will be a moon, but the one thing I want . . . the one thing is missing.

'You will enjoy it. Really you will.' There was a quality in his voice quite different from that in which Tom had encouraged her aunt. Well, so be it. If he would love her there was little that anyone could do about it.

Now Ellie too leant forward, not, as he must have hoped, to speak more closely to him, but to search, and search with a quick furtive need, every face that passed in the street.

The journey was very brief. Soon they heard and felt the rumble of the cab's wheels across the yielding planks of the bridge of boats. They glimpsed the moving lights on the river. Then they were on firm land again. The driver shouted and drew rein. There was an intensified clatter of hooves as the horses drew to a stop. They all climbed out staring into the lighted garden while Eddie Newman gravely paid the driver with money his father had given him.

'There they are,' cried Tom. 'They can only just have

arrived.' Then they all made out the backs of Charles and Marion and the Newmans moving slowly ahead of them deeper into the garden.

It was, as Charlotte had supposed it would be, a place of enchantment. The long thickly leaved branches of the chestnut trees had been trained to reach out and touch one another. Row on row, they stood like dancers in formation, dangling their strings of lanterns against the dark, holding their swaying canopy above them. In the intervals of the music there was a perpetual rustling, for the wind although warm had risen. It plucked at the checked cloths on the tables and sent little whirlpools of dust circling on the worn bare ground. When the orchestra played again it brought the music in gusts like a song sung in an eager breathless voice. Ahead was the lighted bandstand and an open space with couples dancing. Beyond the trees, in the dark intervals backed by the river, red and white lights moved like fireflies.

'How pretty it is,' said Ellie. She slipped her arm through her aunt's and repeated like a lament, 'How pretty it is!'

The orchestra was playing a waltz. It seemed quite suddenly to stop at the height of its frenzy. Applause pattered out from under the trees. The dancers parted. As a party near the bandstand rose to leave they saw Mr Newman move ahead to commandeer their table. Charlotte the automaton, with Ellie leaning on her arm, moved among the tables towards them.

'Come, Charlotte; come, Ellie.' Marion, caught by the poetry of the place, extended her plump arms towards them and gestured them to places in the circle of metal chairs. But she cannot forgive, thought Charlotte; she cannot forget so soon. She sat where she was told, spread her skirts, waited for the gentlemen to arrange themselves, Charles on one side of her, and a moment later, without a word, Edward Newman on the other. The black cuff of his trouser leg, his black boot pale with dust, forced themselves into her vision. She would answer if he spoke to her. Beyond that she had no duty.

But there was no time for conversation. The orchestra was tireless. Before the last couples had left the floor, the music bounded forth again.

'What now?'

She saw Eddie Newman strain eagerly forward as he sat waiting for his elders to make their move. She heard the metal legs of his father's chair grate on the hard ground as he rose, heard his voice which as she had noticed before was deep and not in itself unpleasant. He said as he was bound to do with no lady on the other side of him, 'May I have the pleasure of a dance, Miss Morrison?'

She could meet his eyes with impunity. 'I do not dance.'

'What, not at all?'

'My sister and I have never danced,' said Mr Morrison stiffly.

'And Mrs Morrison? I suppose . . .'

'I should be most pleased,' said Marion.

She rose with a gentle, but especial dignity, for in this one thing she did publicly oppose her husband, pointing out that it was not the dance but the dancers that were prone to sin, and that in that respect he surely knew her to be above temptation. For him and for Charlotte things might be different—besides at their ages it might prove late to learn the dances gracefully—so on her and Ellie rested the duty of setting an example on the floor. He had heard the argument many times. Always he bowed to it, always inexpressibly it pained him.

Edward Newman proferred his arm. His elder son at once stood before Ellie, who rose without so much as a glance at him and allowed herself to be led out onto the floor. Tom bowed elaborately to his mother, who laughed and took his arm. Charlotte was left with Mr Morrison.

His face always appeared stern in repose. How the foolish dancing pained him. Would he speak? Best to wait.

At last he said gloomily, 'Ellie seems happy enough.' Perhaps he supposed an automatic happiness to be one of the perils of dancing, for as he spoke, Ellie's face was drawn past them set against Eddie Newman's dark shoulder and hair, as remote and watchful as if she took no part in what she was doing, scarcely happy.

'Oh, indeed,' said Charlotte, for it was essential that she speak to him in a moderate tone. How absurd he was with his long stand on dancing. His long-felt pain at the sight of his plump defiant wife circling blamelessly in the arms of other men. But if it were not for this rigidity, the stiff seriousness of manner which he could never soften in his dealings with more worldly men, there would be nothing vulnerable in him, nothing to love without awe. She loved him most profoundly under the ironic eye of such a man as Edward Newman. It was unthinkable that she had been angry with him and said what she had said. And in sudden terror that what had passed between them might prove irreversible, she said in a low voice, 'Forgive me.'

'Forgive you for what?' The words were scarcely puzzled. She perceived in them his mind's retreat as surely as if she had heard feet running.

'I raised my voice to you. What I said was inexcusable.'

'You were tired.' How kind he was. How dismissive. 'I have forgotten.'

So that suddenly she was pleading with him, 'Oh, don't forget. Some of what I said must have been true.'

No reply? No reply.

Indeed she felt very tired and that was why it seemed necessary that everything should be explained clearly now while it was still possible to do so. 'Marion was quite just in her accusations. I do dislike Mr Newman. I find it difficult to be civil to him. I know it is quite wrong of me, but I cannot seem to control it.'

The orchestra on its lighted stand had finished the waltz with a flourish. There was a patter of applause and slowly the couples, the younger men still with their arms boldly around their partners' tight waists, still humming the ghost of the tune to which they had danced, were coming back to the tables.

Charlotte made out Ellie and the Newman boy walking more formally arm in arm. His face was grown quite shapeless in a foolish rapturous smile. Poor boy, thought Charlotte. Poor boy.

Behind them she caught sight of Marion and Edward Newman. Immediately she turned away, edging her chair about so as not to catch his eye as he returned to their lighted circle. Thus she found herself looking away from the dancing floor to the circling trees. Here and there single leaves caught the dramatic lamplight and stood out golden. Lamps on the tables flung light up onto faces bent forward towards one another out of the dark foliage, the night spaces between; so happy, so animated, speaking eagerly inaudible words.

It was then that her eye was drawn to a solitary figure leaning against a tree, uniformed, bareheaded, with one leg bent at the knee, one shining boot braced behind him against the narrow trunk, watching intently the dancers move towards their tables. It astonished her to feel joy, reprieve, that her words had lacked the power to send him away.

Had Ellie seen him? Apparently not, although she passed quite close to him. Charlotte glanced at her brother, but he of course would never know him. Even Marion now passed him without a glance, laughing, turning her head up towards Edward Newman. But he disregarded her. His eyes even at that distance sought out Charlotte. She spoke

·

·

rapidly to her brother. 'I should be so very grateful if you would take me back to the hotel.'

'But why?' he said in exasperation, 'when we have been through all this and you had agreed to come.' He did remember then. 'I cannot leave them all when we have only just arrived. Marion would be extremely vexed.'

'Yes,' said Charlotte, 'she would.'

'That was delightful,' said Marion, smiling from one to the other of them, sweeping their voices away with hers. She folded her skirts across her knees as she sat on a metal chair and then spread them out again. Already the orchestra was tuning up for the next waltz. Tom Newman sang aloud in German as he led his mother back to the table.

'Your husband dances most excellently,' Marion said to her. 'I insist that he lead you out as soon as the music starts.' She looked up to where Edward Newman had stood, but he had moved away.

Why, when she cared so little, could nothing distract Charlotte from his movements behind her chair? Now he paced to and fro. Now he stood behind her chair rattling his watch chain as if in indecision. She sat well forward gazing ahead of her. Gazing of necessity at the young Prussian who had moved away from the tree a little into the shadows so that he could stand and stare more freely at the group in which Ellie found her setting.

It was possible to make him out by the lighted cigar he raised and lowered from his lips. It had been so in her dream of the shrubbery. A man at a distance smoking. He seemed to stand there, savouring the sight of them as he tasted the smoke, watching, absorbing, while he could. Ellie, tasted with the eye. No more permitted.

It is his leave, thought Charlotte. He could have gone home to his mother. Instead he has come in this vain pursuit. Tomorrow we go. Perhaps he will wander in the streets for a day or two before he realises, thinking that at any moment she will appear. Then he will give up and rejoin his regiment.

But the pity of his plight was a remote thing. She might have perceived it on the distant bank and reached for her opera glass only to think, there isn't time. It has passed. I shall never understand.

She turned to look at Ellie. Her niece sat with her thin shoulders hunched slightly forward. Her hands were pressed into a fold of skirt between her knees as if she held them there to keep from twisting them. Then, perhaps by the very quality of his looking, her head was raised and turned. She saw and recognised the soldier.

And that too was a distant unobtainable thing to Charlotte watching, although there was no mistaking it. There was a sudden contraction of the slight form on the chair as if at the first painful expulsion of breath. Almost Charlotte expected to hear it issue forth in the coughing wail of birth, but instead there was a powerful joy in the alteration of her face, in the very drawing back of her shoulders and the lift of her head, in the impulse that made Ellie lift her hands from her knees with a small eager gesture towards the dark.

The new waltz had begun in earnest. Poor Eddie Newman, who stood behind her, bent, all unawares of what had happened, to ask her to dance again.

'No.' She turned and smiled quite charmingly at him. No. She was still a little breathless from the last dance. She would sit here a little while longer, just as she was.

Indeed no one seemed inclined to move. Charlotte saw Mrs Newman, presumably at a sign from her husband, smile and shake her head and fan herself with her hand as if in explanation. He stood somewhere behind her. Charlotte heard his foot tap restlessly to the beat of the new waltz. A moment later she felt her chair give and knew that, absently or with some intention, he had let his hand fall on the back of it and now stood leaning some of his weight upon it. The more she escaped him, the more it seemed he pursued.

It was intolerable that she must sit here, a nothing, scarcely even so intentional a thing as a watcher. An instrument to record this man's slightest movement, slightest change of mood. Taut and aware as a divining rod. Ignorant as a stick as to what he might be thinking.

The music grew quite loud. They had chosen especially a table near the band. Now Marion, with her hands clasped delicately to her ears, called across that she wished they had not. It was necessary that everyone raise their voices and edge their chairs closer to the person to whom they spoke. Charlotte, who spoke to no one, stayed where she was. Behind her Edward Newman released his pressure on her chair but did not move away. A moment later he resumed the empty place beside her. He groped in his pocket. She saw that he held and slowly filled a German pipe.

'This is a vile habit, I am told. Even out of doors. But my wife is very tolerant of it. Will it disturb you, Miss Morrison, if I smoke?'

'I am less tolerant. But then I can move away.'

Without looking at her, continuing to concentrate on his own blunt fingers as he tamped the tobacco down into the pipe, he said in a low rapid voice, 'You know that I wish to speak to you where we cannot be overheard. Why are you afraid of me? I shall not take but a moment of your time, but I must explain.'

'I have asked for no explanation.' She actually rose to her feet. But no one took notice of her for at just that moment Ellie too had risen and, smiling delightfully at Eddie Newman, said that she had changed her mind and that she would, after all, very much like to dance. The soldier had made no move towards her. She must now by

·

·

any means available venture out to him. So be it, thought Charlotte, I have done what I could.

Even Mrs Newman roused herself and called out quite gaily, 'I shall change my mind too, Edward. Just until the end of the dance,' and she held out her hands to him in a lazily affectionate gesture as if she needed him alone to raise her from the chair on which she was so comfortably settled. 'Unless,' she added pleasantly, seeing him hesitate, seeing Charlotte standing, 'unless Miss Morrison has relented.'

'Oh, I have not relented,' said Charlotte. She gave no excuse. There was none other than that she wished to be away from them.

She simply walked alone out towards the dancers. She moved among them, ignoring the demands of the music, not caring if they stared: the girls with their high plaits and eyes made round and insolent with excitement. Nor, if the bold young men should smile and make some comment, was she in any danger of understanding what they said. She pushed her way among them until she was well past the tree where the young Prussian waited. With him she had no further business. Then she broke out of the circle of dancers and began to walk rapidly between trees and clusters of chairs.

Now her back was to the warm contrived light of the lanterns. The moon had risen. Coming out from the canopy of trees, she entered its sphere. The tight bitter panic ceased. Moonlight transforms; it deadens; it makes more tolerable. A great shoal of light thrashed on the surface of the river. Everything that stood motionless beside it was rendered in the deepest black. She must not stop. It must be apparent if she walked alone at night that she was impelled by some purpose: that she wanted nothing of anyone. Still it took the breath away: the cathedral fretted at its edges by light. The roof shone like a sheet of silver, each

·

·

tile distinct like the indentation of a hammer. Below the great mass was an illusion. Finally it excluded her, but it was her only landmark; towards it she hurried, first to the bridge and then towards the cathedral.

The barges supporting the bridge were as still as piers. Between them molten light streamed and boiled. The crimson pier lights were cast down into it and shattered their red shafts sliced by the water light, the fragments drawn down sideways, struggling to rejoin, never permitted.

She watched, but all the time she hurried forward. She was on the bridge now feeling under her feet the constant yielding of the planks, for it was crowded with people coming from one bank to the other. She kept to the railing where she could watch the severed lights without ever stopping. All sounds too were fragmented and shaken relentlessly together. The distant orchestra had struck up a polka. There was other conflicting music from somewhere on the river, coming and going in the intervals of the wind, confused voices from the bridge, shouts from a street market, all, like the light, forbidden to join, but shaken and shaken so that no tune was complete, no sentence comprehensible.

None of it concerned her. She would obliterate it all with the thought of the room, the bed, the sound and feel of the key in its lock: its sweet final statement of safety as her wrist turned. And then the warmth and dark of bed. Alone, so that the blankets might cover her head, the knees draw up and press against the body's void.

It was impossible to walk so quickly on the bridge. Several times she had to move away from the rail to avoid some hunched figure staring down into the bright turmoil of water. Then, tightening her shawl and clutching her little purse in her hand, she pushed her way into the busy stream of people. Cabs forced their way past, rattling the planks of the platform. As soon as she might, she made her way back to the railing. In the distance steamer lights wandered as if caught up in some different element. On the bank the black finger of a tower stood up from the water. Just for one moment she allowed her hands to rest on the railing, her head to turn back towards the lighted gardens.

She saw distinctly then in the moonlight the face of Edward Newman. He leant out over the rail as she did but not to look at the river. His purpose was unmistakable. He followed her. She could not see the dark mouth in the whitened face as he called to her.

Instantly she left the rail and began to hurry forward. She dared not look behind, remembering the rapidity of his walk, the suddenness of his appearances, but pressed and pressed forward among the shadowy mass of people.

Away to her left there was a flash of light and over the water came the thud of a gun. A sudden pressure of haste carried her forward. Another flash another thud. Then another. As in nightmares all movement on the bridge began to slow. The crowd ahead thickened. Working her way to the edge again she saw a portion of the black barges carrying their platform break away from the main bridge and float out into the current. The crowd behind pressed in closer. At any moment his voice would strike her. She would feel the infliction of his hand upon her arm. It was possible now to hear the throb of the steamer approach across the water, to see its flaming funnel. She stood still, by the rail, for it to pass.

'Miss Morrison.'

'I do not wish to speak to you,' she said to her hard knuckles on the rail. 'You have no business to follow me. There is nothing that I want of you.'

But he began as if in the middle of the conversation she had denied him. 'You have seen something that you could not have understood.'

.

.

'I have seen nothing. Nothing.' She shut her eyes, the better to concentrate on her anger, forcing the lids tighter and tighter together as if this could buy space between them.

In the blackness she had made, his voice took on a weary patience. 'I have startled you. Forgive me.'

She turned slowly, still gripping the rail, and allowed herself to look at him; to spell out for the last time the features of his face as if they were possessions of hers. Who was he? Standing sideways to her, leaning his arms on the rail, staring grimly down at the water, hunched like the other watchers. Straight nose, full chin, a lock of dark hair. He surrendered her back to the terrors of girlhood, watching Desmond Fermer dancing at Melbury with Sophia Walker. Talking to her. Lifting up his head as he laughed. Oh, she remembered just how. Just like that with a straining of the chin. Poor man. Poor man. How he felt. How he hid his feelings. And she quite lost, thinking does he like me? Does he like me better than Sophia Walker?—turning away from her now so that she could not see his face. The dance was interminable. All these years later she heard it in her head. At supper had she pleased him? Had she displeased him? Was he displeased with how she looked, or with what she had said? That one had been so abject, so wretched and yet had had the resilience to survive. In the last moments he had looked at her in wretchedness and irritation, only anxious to have done with this and be gone. She numbed to what was happening—there had been years to discover what had happened—had felt a confusion of bitterness and pleasure that he was there, that he looked at her at all. So little did she ask. And then he was not there. And she was left asking, Did he love me? Did he go because he had to? Did he go because he had grown tired of it all?

On the shifting bridge above the water in the strange

·

160

·

light Edward Newman said in irritation, 'Is it hopeless to try to speak to you? Shall I leave you here?'

But he must not go. He must speak. He must listen. It was what she wanted. In these last minutes she would not be ignored. He had no choice but to look at her. Do I please him? Do I displease him? And she might freely look at him. The bright steamer approached timing the interval before he might make his escape. So that she said quickly and coldly, 'You were dancing with your wife. Why did you leave her?'

'It was she who saw you go off. She asked me to follow you. She thought you were ill.'

'I am never ill.'

'Well,' he said with a shrug that half apologised for the advantage he had, 'you cannot for the moment get away from me. You must at least listen.'

'Must?' she said. 'Why must?'

'Because you are a danger if you do not.'

'A danger! I intend nothing. I am gone tomorrow.'

'You say you are never ill and I believe you. I believe you were not ill yesterday afternoon when you made your excuses. That you found yourself by some chance sitting in a garden in the city'—here was irony; he must know that she had followed him—'that you saw me meet a lady there.'

She said coldly, watching the steamer, 'Why should you suppose that any of this is of any interest to me?'

His eyes widened. You were interested enough to follow me, he might have said, but he did not, continuing doggedly about his purpose. 'She is the wife of a friend.'

'I do not care who she is. Won't you understand that?'

'You saw me give her something.'

She nodded.

'But you did not see what?'

'I did not trouble.'

'My own, my wife's, my sons' passports.'

·

161

·

'Passports!' She turned slowly to face him. The word with its summer's weight of petty anxieties seemed too alien to accept, as if she had turned two pages together and found a sentence from some other story.

'I beg you to be quiet.' He looked swiftly about him.

She thought, is he afraid? 'Why passports?'

'They must get out of the country. He is in trouble with the police, a political matter. There are two little girls. I was trying to explain this to you yesterday evening. With an English passport they stand some chance. They have left already.'

She said nothing, but stood watching the steamer ply through the gap in the bridge. For a moment its glowing cloud of smoke appeared above the heads of the bystanders. Then it passed through. The missing barges swung slowly back into place.

Was it possible that none of it had been as she thought? She tried to see the scene in the park, the woman's out-stretched arms, the gift pressed into her hands. Had she seen at all what it was? She did not know. But it could not be the truth. She said coldly, 'Your passports were stolen.' But even as she spoke the word it seemed a raft that might drag her back to her old sanity.

He must see how she wanted to believe him. She imagined she saw at the centres of his dark eyes the quickening and brightening of triumph. How they narrowed when he smiled. His face lost its symmetry. The light thrown upon it from the river was filled with uncertainty.

He said, 'They were never in the portmanteau. I had them all along. It seemed a chance to be issued with new ones without arousing any suspicions.'

Was it possible that he could so detach himself from a man's drowning, from his own seeming perfidy, that he could take pleasure in telling her of his cleverness, his

.

162

.

quickness, his resource. Oh, yes. She was not entirely unac-
customed to men.

Under their feet the planks of the bridge jolted. A sigh
of relief, a suppressed cheer, came from the crowd pressing
around them. There was a sudden movement forward, but
without consultation they stayed where they were. The
matter was not entirely resolved.

'What is it you feared of me?' said Charlotte. For fear,
she saw now, was the word that might have explained his
behaviour.

He would not accept it. 'I did not *fear*. Only it occurred
to me that what you had seen was open to quite another
interpretation. I imagined that you might speak to your
sister-in-law, that she might say something to my wife.'

It seemed possible, at least while they stood on the
shifting bridge, to challenge him. 'I did interpret it as you
supposed, but I said nothing.'

'Then I must thank you.'

When she neither spoke nor moved from staring down
at the water, he said a little awkwardly, 'Is there anything I
can do for you? Now. Can I take you back to your hotel?'

But still her mind hankered after certainty. Was it as he
had said it was, or as it had seemed?

'Why could you not simply tell your wife?'

'Because there is a possibility that at the last something
may go wrong; that they may be stopped at Hamburg and
the passports traced back to me. If that should happen, if
we should be questioned; it is essential that my wife and
sons believe absolutely the story they have been told. You
will say nothing?'

'Nothing.' What was there to say? To whom might she
say it?

'Thank you.'

'I wish to return to the gardens.'

.

.

'Certainly.'

With what alacrity did he proffer his arm. Did he then feel reprieved? What did it matter? She too was reprieved. Whatever he was, a gallant friend, a perfidious husband, either or, perhaps, both, he had finally established himself outside her imagination. He was nothing to her. The ghosts he had unwittingly raised were laid. They had no power to haunt her now.

She was walking beside him listening and failing to listen while he talked of his years in Germany. Of his friend, the son of the family with whom he had stayed. How the political passions in a country such as this could never be fully understood in England.

She felt free of a great burden whose weight she had scarcely been aware of until she had set it down. She could have run towards the lighted garden so eager was she about some purpose that she had scarcely defined to herself. And all the time—so oddly the mind veers—she pictured to herself those whitened cottage rooms where she might quietly extend herself, and moving from room to room, meet and recognise herself in forms unaltered by the pressures of others upon her.

When they were among the trees and close to the circle of dancers she slightly pressed his arm and said, 'Won't you join them first. I should like a moment to compose myself.'

'As you wish.'

She watched him walk back, one moment a black shape against the dramatic lantern light, the next he appeared—it seemed by some theatrical trick—set, smiling, among that group of people dearest to her.

As if in some transformation scene they appeared familiar and yet magically altered. Her brother, so well protected from his own inadequacies, not by herself, as she had so wanted to believe, but by his appearance, by his pious-worldly wife. And Marion, with whom she surely could

.

.

not and would not live. It is I that am altered, thought Charlotte.

Would she always see them so? Or as she approached them would they all take up their old positions with one another? No doubt.

There under the hanging lanterns was Ellie whom she loved, unchanged. She knew her purpose. That only was of any importance.

She began to walk rapidly in the direction where she had last seen the Prussian soldier. And surely she did feel light-headed and uncertain of her footing as she approached him. He stood suddenly to attention. He had recognised her. But Charlotte showed no recognition in her turn. Simply she laid her hand upon his arm and, making no appeal to his face, murmured, 'I feel a little faint. Perhaps you would be good enough to escort me to my table. My family is waiting for me.'